T0121070

"VESTIGE AND THE SKIES OF CMAJ."

Joseth Moore

authorHOUSE®

AuthorHouse™
1663 Liberty Drive
Bloomington, IN 47403
www.authorhouse.com
Phone: 833-262-8899

Published by AuthorHouse 03/17/2021

ISBN: 978-1-6655-2023-2 (sc)
ISBN: 978-1-6655-2029-4 (e)

Library of Congress Control Number: 2021905616

Print information available on the last page.

It is a distant future. A generational spaceship becomes a world unto itself. To Maintenance Technician Tyra Housenn and her generation, it's all they've known. Tech Housenn and her search team find an ancient signal on the Ship; an alarm that has existential implications for the colony! How the crew of starship Vestige handles the fuel crisis *and* the colony's 2.5 *million* citizens will be vital to how they approach planet cMaj...

Twenty years later, after the colony is unexpectedly forced to settle on cMaj, all is not well among the humans! The colonial Tribe has broken up into three separate Clans. Now, Tyra's daughter, Miriana, has taken up the mantel of Councilor!

Things are very different with Miriana's generation from her mother's. For humans are in a political competition to build flying air machines. But they are not the only ones in the skies of cMaj!

To my wife and love of my life, Deni; our three children, and the generations after them...and to the Earth.

CHAPTER ONE

Tyra Housenn's internal, cerebral message from her supervisor, Mirandana, auto-connected while Tyra unloaded her vehicle that had dropped her off at the big, old and rusty door to that particular section of the generation-Ship. Big, as in, it was about the size of a two-storey edifice that one would see in the old residential district of the Ship!

Tyra's self-actuator vehicle, with its canopy in lock-down mode, flashed lights and made some audibles to signify to the woman in her twenties that it was about to park off to the side and the human needed to give it some space so she would not get run-over!

"Mirandana, are you *sure* this is where the contractor wants me to check for that signal?" By this time, Tyra had finished unpacking her necessary equipment for her maintenance job. She glanced at one of her info-tools. "By stars' gravity, this portal is so old, it doesn't even register as having been serviced by *any* of the contractors since—"

"Launch date of the Ship," the older woman said over their cerebral-comm. "Yeah, I did a little research on it before the business had me send you over...If you have trouble getting it open, request succor from the synthetics."

Tyra tsked sarcastically. "We have some explosives that'll do the job!"

A shared laugh…

"The Company has allotted your payments for a full day's worth—*maximum*, Tyra. So, don't get in too much of a hurry where you hurt yourself *or* damage the ship, affirmed?"

The Ship-maintenance crewmember wasn't quite finished yet. "If it's so important, why are they having a main-tech search for this signal? Shouldn't some official from one of the engineering schemes do this?"

Tyra could see over the cerebral-comm that her boss showed some apprehension, despite herself. But she merely shrugged. "Corporation gods don't tell me the details… I'm guessing they have a lot of bigger projects they have to deal with—like making sure our home-Ship doesn't run out of energy. Or making sure we can withstand the *next* meteor storm! To *them*, sending engineering over to look for some unexpected signal deep in the *original* sector of the Ship would be a little too much like playing archaeology…"

"Digging a little *too* deep in history, is it," Tyra quipped as she approached the towering slab of the pitted and dusty metallic door. Various layers of texts and labels from long-ago generations had intermittently graffitied the portal. "And you've wondered why I've never dated an engineer!"

A chuckle from her over-visor. "I'm guessing it's

just some ancient proximate-reader for a business that's long-dead."

That caused Tyra to pause in her tracks. "But to read *what*? However long it's been since our Ship voyaged out of our solar system and got barnacled with asteroids, our ancestors had no idea *where* they were going...so why would they need a proximate-timer?"

"Like I said—*too much archaeology for the engineers...* that's why we have *you* there!"

The main-tech shook her head. "Stars, I love a mystery! Ok, boss; message received...I previously checked all messaging and visuals to ensure functionality parameters are standard, and same goes for my synth-tools and computerables..."

"Ok, that's an affirmed—contact me *directly* if something weird happens!"

And their implanted comms were disengaged.

One Hour Later...

Tech-Housenn was finally getting to the point where the heavy, house-sized door was beginning to shutter from all her synthetic-labors' work of using heat with some oils to get the port sliding! That is, *after* she had programmed her synths to scrape away at all the rust that had cemented the door!

"Tech-Housenn," one of the synthetics had audioed over the shrieking of metal scraping against metal as the port nudged, "it is recommended that only five feet is needed for you to passage the port!"

She gave a terse nod. "That would be the most logical approach," she said over the noise as the other synthetic labors continued to coat the threshold of the huge portal with industrial grease as their mechanical grappling arms forced the looming door to open. Again, just a few feet.

And suddenly, there was silence after the synths finished moving the door… Silence, but for a faint gust of humid, stuffy air that escaped the other side of that time capsule!

While she was reading her portable computerized equipment, Tyra barked out telemetry for the recording. "Oxygen has been slightly burned up in there—nineteen percent; nitrogen, *eighty* percent…carbon dioxide approaching *two-tenths of a percent*!…methane just short of *thirty-thousandths*!"

Tyra ponderously looked up from her reader and peered into the darkened side of the portal while the recording kept going. Her computerable device interjected the obvious.

"Tech-Housenn, something has been *using* the air during the eon *since* the commencement of the Ship's voyage!"

Silence…more moistened air breezing by the main-tech and her small synthetic crew…

"That's impossible!"

"Apparently not," one of the boxy, somewhat anthropomorphic, synthetics said dryly.

"Synths," Tyra put to her three mechanicals, "would *now* be a good time to contact Supervisor Ellisante? She said to do so—*directly*—if we ran into anything weird…I would classify this as weird!"

Surprisingly, there was a pause among the synths!

"Perhaps it would help if we were to scan for any life forms *first*," one of the synths volunteered. "With such a vast space vehicle, it is possible that an enclosed section within the Ship *could* usurp the original air that was contained after your ancestors decided to close off this section of the Ship."

There was a series of audibles from Tyra's portable device. "Tech-Housenn, I took advantage of your conversation and scanned for life signs and have found *none*—with the exception of mere traces of micro-organisms that normally reside in an urban ecosystem dominated by humans."

She frowned; slightly relaxing her tense posture. "So, basically, no life signs?"

"That is correct," the portable responded.

"Tech-Housenn," another of the three synths input, "it is possible that the aggregate-effects of such germs are responsible for the relatively off-kilter readings; especially over such vast amounts of time."

There was a chorus of, '*Indeed*,' between the two other synths and the tech's portable device!

This caused Tyra to feel a lot better, as she nodded to herself. "Affirmed, then…I say we go locate that proximate-timer and get this job done!"

More synthetic affirmations from the synths and her portable. All the synths turned on a built-in light that each harbored; flooding the immediate area behind the portal with electrifying light! But a few seconds after the mechanical laborers and the human stepped through the grand portal, Tyra had a thought as she looked back at the partially opened door behind them.

"I don't care which one of you, but I'd like one of you synths to stand guard on the *other* side of the portal…

you never know when an emergency might come up and *one* of us should be on the *outside* of that gigantic door!"

Without a word, one of the synths simply turned and smoothly gaited toward the slit of light coming through the portal's hatch...

As the rest of the team cautiously walked further into the cavernous section—the light cast from the two remaining laborers—Tyra finally got to *see* just how *big* the enclosed section of her generational Ship was...Tyra's portable had already scanned the entire sector: well over a million square-feet! One of the synths projected a three-dimensional rendering of the layout of the sector, demarking where the search team was at each second. The overall design of the sector was a bit irregular, in shape. A multitude of compartmentalization—from rooms the size of a simple abode to caverns about a third of that one million square-feet! And as big as that was, main-tech Tyra had to remind herself that the closed-off sector was merely *one-fifth* of the entire generation-Ship that they all were passengers on...

Not surprisingly, the very cultural *feel* of that sector of the generational ship was from a vastly *different* era from Tyra Housenn's generation. Indeed, while they continued to search for the enigmatic signal, Tyra, the two remaining synths, and her portable device, *all* had pointed out from time to time the various spots where they could see how Tyra's ancestors had constructed and expanded upon the original Ship's layout.

Some parts the small team could tell where the very conception of the Ship itself—the infrastructure and superstructure looked more jumbled with rivers of conduit pipes, perhaps, a hundred feet across *each*! And as one looked back *toward* the giant portal, where the search team came from, they were able to tell there were several more years of advanced technology by the time the ancestors had built the looming portal!

How the ancients of Tech-Housenn's people did this, even the synths and the portable computerable had no viable reference to.

Which, of course, led to the obvious question that needed to be spoken aloud…

"So, why would my ancestors close this sector off from the rest of the Ship," Tyra put out to any of the computerables.

"And also, Tech-Housenn," her portable said, "about what timeline did they do this? We've been in this cordoned sector for a while, now, and I've yet to see *any* signs of a conflict or an emergency…"

All went quiet as they thought on the questions that were just posed. And then—

"Tech-Housenn," one of the synths exclaimed; it's boxy figure quickly swiveled toward another section of the cavern, "I've got the signal!"

"Good job…could you take us there?"

"Ma'am!" Using one of the benefits in being a synthetic being, the synth snapped out wheels from beneath its feet and quickly rolled toward where it had found the signal! The other synth of the search party had done the same with its wheels. The human hurried behind both the best she could; her light source emanating from her portable!

The two synths rolled straight into a relatively small section that would've been considered a "suite" in ancient times. There were no doors, so it was easy access for all to start looking around the collection of rooms…

"Right here, Tech-Housenn!" This was the other synth.

The two synthetics and the human all converged upon some ancient form of a console. Impossibly, the only instrument working in all the ruins was that flashing, alternating colorful light!

"I suggest touching it, someone," Tyra's portable prompted in the frozen awe!

One of the synths took the portable's suggestion… A high-pitched whirring sound followed and was gone in a few seconds. The flashing light on the console was the same colors, though it glowed a solid light now.

Suddenly, a flash of light winked on in front of them—startling the human! The two synths were surprised, but not startled as the biological being was next to them. That light originated from a large, rectangular surface; smooth and made of glass—or something similar. And within that lit rectangular, flat object were, unmistakably, letters! Indeed, words… Maintenance Tech Tyra Housenn had heard about such ancient systems of communicating before, when she was a little girl growing up in the rotating, cylindrical sector of the Ship. The ancients called such system Writings, or Words…

Accompanying the strange squiggles was a rather severe, flashing picture—an image, of some thin piece of line that was animated. As if that slender needle were quivering. And above *it*, in addition to that Writing, there were a series of, yet, smaller lines—a bit more blocky, and arranged in an arching fashion.

Tyra checked to make sure her visuals were still recording, and they were. "How curious!"

"…Tech-Housenn—" one of the synths started.

"—isn't this wonderful, everyone!" She flashed a smile and was truly giddy! "We are witnessing, in real-time, how the ancients communicated with each other! In *our* era, we've been using icono—"

"—Tech Housenn," this time, the other synthetic laborer tried.

"—and I'll send this experience today to the major societal journals…perhaps that's what our ancestors were doing when they abandoned this sector: keeping a kind of *reserve* for how—"

"—Maintenance Tech Housenn," her portable actually *yelled* at her! Obviously, the computerable had gotten her attention. "One of the things we, computerables—including your synths—are programmed for is some basic cultural information. Of course, from contemporary times to most of antiquities… This projection is a deeply disturbing message for *every* single being residing within the Ship…"

Just before Tyra could respond, one of the synths interjected. "Tech-Housenn, it translates into, *Running Low…*"

The maintenance tech *still* did not comprehend. "Low on what?"

"*Fuel*, Tech-Housenn," her portable came back in the dialogue. "Apparently, your ancestors had found some kind of fuel where a civilization could run off it for thousands of years."

"*Nuclear*, I believe is what they called it," the other synthetic input.

"Nuclear…" the human repeated, "nuclear—I've heard of it! In history, we studied how…"

Her eyes drifted to some corner of the chamber.

"Yes, Tech-Housenn," the portable said softly, "I think you've figured out and completed the task your contractor has given you…your ancestors used this nuclear to power this generational ship for an eon, but in doing so, there, apparently, was an accident. Ma'am, there was a very good reason *why* your ancestors closed off this sector from the rest of the Ship…"

Now, it was silent between the two synthetic beings, the portable computerable that was attached to Tyra's upper-left arm, and the young female human…silent except for the ancient electronic alarm—though no longer beeping since one of the synths had engaged the alarm button, but there was a constant *humm* in place.

"Radiation, Portable," she asked the small device; half-way *not* wanting to hear the answer!

"That, Maintenance Tech Housenn, is actually the *good* news here, today…apparently so much time has gone by since whatever event it was that may have triggered your ancestors' abandonment of this sector, that the radiation levels are negligible! Though there are trace-amounts. I'd venture to suggest that we not stay here much longer, Tech-Housenn; just to be safe."

"Agreed!"

"Tech-Housenn," one of the two synthetic laborers asked as the team started to turn around to head back to the large portal, "are we to shut the door behind us? It would seem to be the most logic to do; given what we've learned here."

The young woman slightly flinched upon hearing the question—apparently, she had not thought of that!

"That *would* be the obvious, precautionary thing to do, synth...synthetic Number Two," she called out over her comm-device to the mechanical that had voluntarily gone back to the portal to stand guard, "we're on our way back."

"Indeed, Tech-Housenn...I've been observing the reconnaissance team all this time. And I hope you don't mind, Maintenance Tech Housenn, but I've taken the liberty to contact Supervisor Ellisante of the mission. Including connecting the simultaneous-feed of the mission...by the time the four of you arrive, there should be a safety-evaluation crew here to look you all over for any radiation."

"Affirmed that, synth Two. And thank you..."

CHAPTER TWO

The Office of Infrastructure held an emergency meeting that same day, facilitated by one of the Ship's main self-actuator computerables; hours after Synthetic laborer Two had zipped Maintenance Technician Tyra Housenn's reconnaissance within the Ship's cordoned sector *to* Supervisor Mirandana Ellisante. It was not the entire employee-body of the Office, but of those who were in the major decision-making positions within the Ship.

Generations earlier, the charges of the Office of Infrastructure had the foresight to re-locate the agency within the middle section of the twenty-miles long spacecraft—that way the Office was equidistant from all sections of the Ship and travel-time was kept to a minimum! The *outer* hull of the Ship, Vestige, had *originally* been a smooth, elongated craft. But over the eon of its traversing outside Earth's solar system ended up being encrusted with meteors and asteroid debris.

However, given that Infrastructure was *not* located *within* the coveted O'Neillian cylinder sector of the Ship— mostly reserved for residential and more professionally academic zones, the Office had a bit of a low reputation… that their whole agency *was* maintenance, as opposed to maintenance being a division *within* the Infrastructure agency. With help from the Ship's myriad of science and engineering organizations *and* the Ship's own self-actuator, Infrastructure was the agency that *logistically* was the one in charge of maintaining that five-mile-wide, spinning colony of two-and-a-half or so *million* residents of the entire generational ship that people took for granted!

Given the centerpiece of the problem was the nuclear fuel that was powering the Ship had finally reached the threshold of minimal-operational levels, scores of scientists from various disciplines had, also, attended the emergency meeting. Since the current actuator computerable was a relatively new manufactured system programmed *by* much older systems some decades previously, it was the main reason *why* the Ship's systems were not aware of the nuclear fuel issue…in an ancient way of putting it: nuclear energy being the very source of power *for* the island-sized ship was *Lost in Translation* during the reboot of the Ship's central systems those decades ago!

Even though she was considered low on the rung within Infrastructure, Main Tech Tyra Housenn, also, sat in on the meeting, as did her supervisor, Ellisante—*All Hands On Deck*, was another of the ancient aphorisms that was applicable.

The meeting, at that point, had been going on for about thirty minutes and scientists, engineers, and maintenance workers were *still* showing up—info devices on hand, as the late-comers pulled up a chair to the packed kiosk-tables, stationed close to each other…

"…twenty more years left," Maintenance Garson

Hanway retorted; his head swiveling around as he looked at the large group around the different kiosk-tables. "By your cerebral-message, I thought we were about to sputter to a halt in a few *days*!"

Agreements were voiced around the media-tables… Tyra quietly noticed that *none* of them were from any of the scientists.

"Maintenance Hanway," Chemist Poul Ean replied in a bit condescending tone, "for a *generational* ship, we're fortunate to have had *this* much time to figure out how to deal with our fuel supply…as much time it takes for the logistics of trying to find the closest planet or moon for us to park next to and orbit; *then* you have to think about sending out scouting missions to those planets; and, of course, all the while we have to *keep* feeding and facilitating almost three *million* residents while we do this!"

"Indeed, Maintenance Hanway, twenty years is not a lot of time to deal with our dwindling ship-fuel," computerable physicist, Ellenain Eshe, put to the maintenance worker. She, then, turned her attention to the whole group at all the kiosk-tables—looking through projections of iconographic data that also depicted a diagram of the asteroid-encrusted ship at each table. (Ever since Tyra and her search team found that ancient signal, she had been more mindful how *her* generation communicated exclusively with pictographs. With the exception of math expressions.) "I'd like to hear from the Ship's rotating crew…You all know more than anyone else of the history the last time the Ship had made port on a planet or moon…whether or not we've had energy surges…I guess what I'm asking is, Do we have enough energy from this nuclear thing for us to even *look* for a planet to dock with and utilize *its* natural resources?"

"—Great question!"

"—Stars, we're in trouble if we even have to ask that!"

"—I heard a computerable report say something like a hundred years ago!"

"—Shouldn't that be in our records?"

"Ok, let's hear from the Ship's crew," Yeo, an engineer, suggested as she did a sweeping gesture with one of her hands.

The ancient ship's main crew were scattered among the other people at the kiosk-tables, but it was evident who they were by the way they glanced at one another to see who'd speak among them, *for* them.

Billamont Harvester, one of the Ship's rotating crew members, cleared his throat and, apprehensively, responded. "A few of us were discussing this while on the way here over our cerebral-comms…and you are actually on the point, Physicist Eshe, about the need to divert the Ship to an astronomic body in order to compensate our fuel-loss…"

"Why do I hear a, *But*, coming from you, Crew-Harvester," Astrophysicist Cairo an Preun pointed out from across the headquarters' conference hall. He kept his eyes on the shipmate while everyone else shifted in their respective seats to get a look at Billamont.

The shipmate's eyes uneasily flitted to his crewmates scattered around those media-tables before he responded. "Look, you can't expect a ship that started off with some thousands of residents thousands of years ago to ignore the issues related to *that* ship's fuel supply…years ago, we Crewmembers *did* discuss—more speculation, really—what we might have to do *should* the Ship run into some near-fatal incident with one of those meteor storms. Back then, when I was a new recruit, some of the elders suggested that we scrap our long-held philosophy of drifting about in space in a big ship and just *find* a habitable planet or moon to settle onto…"

There was a stir that began among some within the large meeting. Crew-Harvester went on.

"Well, like I said, it was more idle speculation than a serious policy to look into…" He shrugged, in a defeatist way, main tech Tyra noticed. "And that was pretty much it, sisters and brothers…it was kind of a sore spot to discuss this—almost political! Sadly, some of the crewmembers back in my young days as a shipmate wanted nothing to do with migrating to a planet or moon. I don't know…I guess one could've called them a kind of 'purist' movement within the Ship's crewmembers. You know; what's the point in constructing a generational ship just to dock it within a geo-centric orbit around, yet, another planet…?"

There were some tacit nods to that point, but the majority of the engineers, scientists, and even among the maintenance workers, were all looking upon Crew-Harvester with suspicious eyes! This was not lost on him.

"I guess the thrust of what I'm saying is, even though I, personally, was open to looking to settle onto a planet—and a few other crewmembers—the majority of the rotating crew were *not*! Between that mindset of the Ship's crew *and* our updated actuator systems *not* configuring the older systems with the programming of the nuclear fuel *with* them..." Now Crew-Harvester, in earnest, looked around at everyone in the conference hall, seated at those kiosk-tables. "*This* is how we got into this mess, apparently!"

For the first time of the emergency meeting, there was a ruckus!

"I ask that all in attendance please be respectful and keep all interactions courteous," the Ship's synthetic voice sternly put; its audible booming above. No doubt, there was some psychology at play in such gesture!

"You realize we've passed *two* planets since you've been a recruit, Crew-Harvester," maintenance tech Bennie Dotansk put to all the rotating shipmates as she looked around the gathering.

There was a chorus of consent, as the attendees tried measuring their responses after the warning from the Ship's actuator!

"What's the next planet the Ship will run across," Geologist Fillip Natsome threw out to anyone.

"We've been in the periphery of the Canis Major Dwarf minor-galaxy for the past three years now," the Ship's actuator answered before any human scientists had a chance of even thinking on the subject! "During the era when the Ship was originally constructed, humans did not know a lot of details of the Virgo Supercluster, much less the planets *within* those galaxies..."

Just then, the Ship's actuator changed the projected iconographics hovering above the center of each kiosk-table. The projection *now* featured a colorful rendering of the irregular galaxy the Ship had just crossed into a few years ago. Icono-telemetry floating about, depicting where the Ship was and the various galaxy in the astronomic cluster.

"Even now," the audible continued as the computerable enlarged the Canis Major system's graphics, "we still have not given proper names to these systems...but to answer your question, Geologist Natsome, there *is* one planet in the Ship's current trajectory, and it has *potential* hospitable conditions for humans!"

There were gasps of hope among those attending the emergency meeting—some even tearing up.

"Mind you, it *is* nearly one year *out* from us at the Ship's current velocity," the audible actuator qualified, but this did not seem to dissuade the humans!

At that point, the colorful projection enlarged even further and depicted a relatively large planet with three small moons orbiting it. "We've utilized the Bayer nomenclature of deep-antiquities, but for *this* planet, and we've designated it as *cMaj*—named after the Canis Major system...conversely, the air is a bit thick for humans— oxygen levels is around twenty-*five* percent and since it's a much bigger terrestrial planet than where humans originated from, the gravity *and* the atmosphere are a lot heavier than you would like—"

"I recommend we *increase* the speed of the terrestrial cylinder to match the gravity of cMaj," Astrophysicist Keyton venBot blurted out; optimism on his countenance—also, he stood straight up from his chair while doing so! "That way our sisters and brothers of the Ship can acclimate to the planet!"

There were applauds upon Astrophysicist venBot's suggestion!

"That is highly recommended, Astrophysicist venBot," the stern actuator of the Ship commented. "I might also recommend we do the same to match the atmospheric makeup of cMaj...are there any objections from the humans attending this meeting?"

Everyone in the conference room looked around and just about every one of them shook their heads; having no objections. The way things were governed on the ancient generational ship was mostly communal. But de facto, the Ship's actuator systems functioned as the leader of that human-communal organization of scientists, engineers, maintenance crew, and the various civilian and military agencies that ran the ancient society on a daily basis.

The generational Ship was not a democracy; nor was it an autocratic system. It simply seemed logical to the humans within that asteroid-sized ship to *let* the computerable system take the lead on, literally, steering the ship of humans that would prove too complicated for them!

"We'll need to come up with a media campaign," Mirandana Ellisante, Tyra's boss, threw out to the group. She directed her attention to a group of professionals seated at a kiosk-table a bit further back...most of them were from the *civilian* agencies that dealt with human health-related subjects and societal issues. "It probably would be nice to have projected mediums *and* personal-public engagements about the upcoming changes to the cylindrical sector of the Ship—so the populace won't be afraid and would have time to adjust."

There were several affirmations from the group, the

optimism from the meeting emanating from the civilian professionals as well.

"Do we really need to tell them," Dambudzo, a well-known psychologist, curtly put to the meeting. There was an uncomfortable silence after her question, but she continued. "Trust me, sisters and brothers, in *my* field we have a long history of humanity acting as a river of consciousness that is not necessarily bad; *but* nor is it necessarily *good*! I wonder how an enclosed spaceship of two-and-a-half-million people will behave when they've learned we are *low* on fuel for the very thing that's kept them *and* their civilization alive for an eon!"

Once again, there was a stir in the large meeting.

"Psychologist-Dambudzo," this time it was main tech Tyra Housenn that decided to jump in, "are you suggesting that we wait until the Ship is *closer* to cMaj a little less than a year from now, or that we do not tell the populace at all?"

"I say we never tell them at all!" Again, a stirring among the large group of humans at the various kiosk-tables. The psychologist tried to clarify for them. "Remember some of the more recent political movements we've had with some in society…like the group that tried to convince all of the elderly in the populace to commit euthanasia so they could make *more* room for the younger citizens on the Ship! How many of our elderly had we lost to those avaricious idiots?"

"Hundreds," main tech Housenn responded grimly; given that she was the one to question the psychologist.

Psychologist-Dambudzo gave a terse nod. "Indeed, Maintenance Technician Housenn, many speculate that *some* of those suicides were not suicides at *all*! And, now, we're going to tell those very same people our planet-ship is about to run *out of fuel* in just two decades…"

The psychologist's retort was poignant. Indeed, Tyra was able to see that she was the perfect fit for such profession!

"Psychologist-Dambudzo raises a very important issue," the Ship's actuator audible came back into the meeting. "Shall this gathering inform the greater-populace of the nuclear fuel issue or not?"

It was with this issue that the humans in charge of running the generational Ship truly found complicated! They all looked around their respective kiosk-tables; uncertain how they should respond!

"Perhaps the humans should vote on it—via the raising of hands?" the actuator asked.

The large group of humans, as if demonstrating that river of consciousness that Psychologist-Dambudzo had just addressed, automatically fell in line.

"All *for* informing the populace," the Ship's audible system stated—approximately one-third of the governing humans voted *for* it with upheld hands.

"All for *not* informing the populace…" This time, the *two-thirds* that did *not* vote with the first group all held up their hands.

A bit of mumbled conversations after the vote, but the actuator went on. "It is official, then…the attendees of this meeting *must* respect the vote of this governing body by its majority. I've recorded the vote—indeed, the whole proceedings—so it is incumbent on *each* member *not* to inform the greater population of this ship's dwindling fuel."

That included maintenance tech Tyra Housenn... whom, in fact, voted *to* inform the public...

CHAPTER THREE

A Time...

The four-star systems within the Canis Major irregular galaxy had been gradually getting brighter—from the perspective of the residents of the generational Ship—for close to a year at that point. Many residents, *at first*, had not noticed the subtle changes in the gravitational-spinning colony, as the centrifugal speed slightly *increased*. Or that the artificial air had become richer—emergency crews all over the colony had noticed a marked increase in bigger fires within buildings and even in a few open-air fields where farming colonists *swore* they made sure to shut down their machinery to ensure nothing caught on fire. Such was due to the scientists within the governing organization pumping in a bit *more* oxygen, so that the Ship's artificial air would gradually match that of planet cMaj.

There, actually, *were* educated and suspicious citizens that *had* noticed. There was a small movement of residents organizing themselves within their local sectors; forming what amounted to monitoring organizations that were counterbalances to the Ship's *official* governing organization! But the actuator system dispatched an army of infiltrators to *all* those groups. The various agents within those local citizen organizations did a good job in tampering down many of the locals' suspicions and monitoring of the Ship's governance.

All that worked perfectly for the Ship's government of its actuator systems and its large groups—or, "nodules"—of human professionals...But then came the news over Maintenance Technician Tyra Housenn's personal media kiosk at her abode, within the immense, spinning colony's residential sector...

The projection's event-alert—as was custom for news of Tyra's generation—was simple: it showed several pictions of various citizens, while in the background a moving piction of the event itself. Iconographics hovered, giving brief but poignant details of the event, and the news-alert was over...

That is to say, the news being the *storming* of the Office of Infrastructure's headquarters by a large mob of residents that had enough of a year's-worth of changes in the colony's ecosystem and being told it was all in their heads!

"My stars," Tyra blurted out to herself in her one-person residence. She looked around her abode; feeling a pit in her stomach after remembering that almost a year ago, the Ship's governing-nodes of its actuator systems and the circles of human professionals had voted to keep the citizens of the Ship in the dark about the Ship's dwindling supply of nuclear energy...and now, as a consequence of that vote nearly a year ago, a large portion of the Ship's citizenry were suspicious of their governing-nodules and were, *now*, pretty much at an official revolutionary stage!

As Tyra quickly dressed herself from a simple domestic gown to a public attire, her own residential actuator inquired, in a female voice to match the resident living within, "Tyra, do you think it is a good idea to go out tonight, with the uprising at Infrastructure's headqu—"

"It's all the reason *more* for me to go, Home-Synth! I've never told anyone else—not even *you*—but I have *some* responsibility, in my own way, of what's happening tonight!"

"I see…then I bid you good fortune, Maintenance Technician Tyra Housenn. I only *hope* I will see you again."

Tyra knew it was the actuator's way of trying to discourage her from going out. And it did not work…

She lived in a section within the Cylinder that was a bit further out from the center of the spinning, circular landscape of open lands and intermittent clusters of towns that were strategically scattered from each other…again, thank the ancestors for having the foresight to design a balanced planet-like ecosystem! But that was all deceptive, really, Tyra could now truly see…

Being a bit farther away also meant Tyra had to contract a vehicle from one of her local township's mass-transit division. For during the artificial night-cycle there weren't a lot of commuting land- nor air-transportation doing their pre-programmed routes. Given she was, obviously, in a hurry, Tech-Housenn ordered a single-flyer that was not much bigger than two adults put together!

She conducted her purchase at the kiosk of the transportation depo of her town, hopped into her leased single-flyer, selected her destination, and the vehicle zipped off into the colony's artificial night sky; joining a traffic of flitting transporters already lighting the night…

CHAPTER FOUR

The Infrastructure agency's offices were much further down the central section of the Ship itself—away from the glitzy O'Neillian sector. Indeed, the Office of Infrastructure had moved to that strategic middle-section for logistical purposes generations ago as the Ship's population grew, and those earlier generations of residents had expanded the Ship's configuration. As far as Tech-Housenn's generation could tell from some of the ancient records, those earlier generations had "docked" the Ship at a geo-centric orbit for a couple of asteroids and utilized their elements by mining them for building-materials...

That same Office that had spearheaded such lofty engineering feats those generations ago was *now* under attack by several *thousand* of the Ship's citizens!

Maintenance Tech-Housenn was jostled among the horde of mostly younger people as she plowed her way through the knot! Along with human security, there was a battalion of tall synthetics that were of the specialty design—their specifications being more hardy and intimidating looks to mostly scare off rioting citizenry.

The captain of the enforcement forces recognized Tech-Housenn from previous businesses within the

Ship. Standing next to him on the balcony, as they monitored the situation, were three nodule-members—Psychologist-Dambudzo, Shipmate Billamont Harvester, and Astrophysicist-Keyton venBot. Captain Marcus Sommerst got all three's attention and pointed her out to them. They all flinched with surprised gasps at seeing the small, young woman within the boiling crowd as she clearly was having trouble trying to reach them!

The captain spoke into his comm-device and one of the militarized synth's jets fired up and it flew over and then *into* the mob—rioters scattering just before it virtually crash-landed right in front of Tech-Housenn! The synthetic then grabbed Tyra and flew back over to the elevated section of the facility, joining Captain Sommerst and the three nodule-members. The synth stood by, waiting for Captain Sommerst's next orders before it flew off to join the other synthetic enforcers.

"Don't hurt them, Captain," Tyra called out to him over the clamor as more of the towering synthetic beings were ordered by the captain to go out into the crowd and box them in! "They're just frustrated about the living conditions we've imposed on them!"

Nodule members Dambudzo and Harvester both looked upon the young maintenance technician with appraising eyes, then glanced at each other but kept their thoughts to themselves.

"Where are some of the other nodule members," Tyra asked any of the others nearby.

"We advised them to stay away after it started to turn *this* ugly," Astrophysicist-venBot explained. "We didn't expect *you* to come, otherwise we'd have sent you the same message, Tech-Housenn!"

"I was part of that meeting; I feel I should help!"

The scientists gave her a *different* appraising look from that of his colleagues. Respect...

The riot suppression by the synths was successfully walling off the rioters from the Infrastructure's facilities, pushing the crowd down toward a more open area of the Ship's interior.

"Of course, you know what this means," Psychologist-Dambudzo put to the small group; all turning their attention to her. "This will be the start of the latest movement, of a long *list* of movements, of this ship's very long history!"

The three other nodule members and the captain either nodded their heads or quietly absorbed the words of the psychologist.

"Hold them there," Captain Sommerts said to his forces via his hidden comm, "let some of their agitation run its course...if they're as logical as they're portraying themselves to be, they'll think otherwise and disperse without *us* having to take them into custody!"

Tyra could see from their high position on the balcony the seven-foot tall synths gradually form a mechanized wall of enforcers, and on the other side, the thrashing rioters. Some, she noticed, were gesturing to the nodes on the balcony—placing their hands over their throats, as if someone were choking them! An apparent reference to, in fact, the Ship's scientists releasing a higher level of oxygen and other elements into the Ship's artificial air; thinking it would do the populace some good to acclimate them to their up-coming dock with planet cMaj...

Which, by the way, the governing node-government, along with the Ship's actuator system, had *yet* to tell the colonists about...and when they eventually do, they all knew, the *real* trouble with the populace would happen! Psychologist-Dambudzo's words of a new movement were, indeed, poignant...

CHAPTER FIVE

Days had passed since the uprising of thousands of the Ship's citizens at the Office of Infrastructure. Maintenance Technician Housenn had a day off from her official vocational duties, and she was determined to investigate the Ship's situation with its depleting nuclear fuel all on her own! There were some things about the situation with the Ship's history that seemed a bit patchy and Technician Housenn didn't want to chance it to a group of professionals that were not likely to be cooperative with such missing data.

She was among the youngest of the governing nodule-government, from the Maintenance node of that system. So, frankly, she was not taken that seriously among most within that governing body. Tyra saw it. She did a good job of ignoring the looks from the older and/or more educated within the nodules' disciplines, especially during the large meetings the nodule would hold for Ship-businesses. Hence, why she packed her torso-strapped computerable and her personal technical equipment and quietly set out for the enclosed area of the Ship during the colony's night cycle!

As her portable device told her the first time, when she

had gone in nearly a year ago, the radiation from whatever incident happened with the nuclear had mitigated to the point of moderate levels. She didn't want to risk even low levels of *any* kind of radiation, but her portable explained to Tyra that the half-life breakdown of the enclosed sector's radiation levels were to the point that she could spend up to two days inside—but no more than that!

Again, before she flew off to the ancient sector of the Ship, Tyra's personal actuator at her home tried convincing Tyra not to go—it was a maternalistic/paternalistic synthetic-programming that her parents had *personally* created for her when she left on her own from their household. They wanted, at the very least, a portion of themselves with her after she had graduated to adult status a couple of years ago and moved out on her own.

One of the advantages in working for the Office of Infrastructure was one had access to maintenance portals that were not meant for the average citizens to go through. Maintenance Tech Housenn utilized her knowledge of that network of maintenance, subterranean portals so that she was able to evade the Ship's security tech-observers and its foot-patrol of synth guards...Technically speaking, Tech-Housenn was not breaking the law, but, rather, *protocols* when she gained access to that ancient enclosure via *another*, much smaller portal that she found.

This time, with no synthetic laborers to help her, she utilized her technician's tools to loosen up and opened the ancient portal—*this* one, about the size of a personal-hatch meant for emergency exiting, she speculated. Tyra made sure to quietly close the tiny hatch behind her so that no one would notice...

With all of her equipment attached on her person, or hooked onto her service-belt, Tyra had her portable engage its flood lights *and* bring up a permanent projection of diagrams of where they were in the one million-plus square feet ancient section. She took some time to examine the projection of the enclosed section of the Ship and decided to go a different route from her first incursion into the darkened and, oddly, clean ruins.

As she made her way through the sectioned-Chamber, Tech-Housenn saw more of those odd characters posted throughout the walls and postings—those Letters, Words, and some type of iconographics of *their* ancient times that reminded Tyra of her generation's system of communication. But a different "dialect" of iconography...what were those odd, geometrical shapes with the Writings for? Some were stark-red. Others, yellow... Green was another color she saw constantly in the ancient posts and signs.

As she was spellbound by the history and archaeological contents of her informal investigation of the Ship's nuclear depletion, Tyra kept finding even *more* historical artifacts and sections within the eon's old chamber that stole her attention from her mission! One was a section that was recessed into the walls of the Chamber and seemed to function as some kind of public teaching facility. For there were large, still images within rectangular frames hanging on the walls of this section—*Paintings*, as she remembered from her history classes. Paintings of people from those ancient times of humanity; when they had *first* taken to other astronomical bodies and began to trek *outside* of what was called *Mother Earth* by some and began

33

to colonize the solar system that was thousands of years *behind* Tyra's generation's Ship…

She stopped to looked at the paintings, specifically of the ancestors. They were of varying ethnic families, but clearly humans hadn't change all that much in all the thousands of years! The clothing and how humans expressed their cultures, of course, *did* change a lot…

"Founders of the Ship," Tech-Housenn speculated to her portable device in the stark silence; a slight echo in the Chamber.

A pause from the portable. "Given the attention to display these portraits in this public forum's space, it would seem so, Tech-Housenn…So much of our Ship's history was lost from so many changes in the Ship's actuator's programming, not even the computerables can even give accurate speculation on many of these ancient, cultural sites!"

The last statement gave Tech-Housenn an idea. "Portable, is it possible for you to catalogue *all* of the characters and iconographs you've seen—from our first trip here a year ago, to today, and *then* try to run some kind of estimate-translation of the Ancients' language?"

There was no pause from the device for that question! "Indeed, Tech-Housenn…I hope you don't mind, but I've already *started* to do that!"

She chuckled with a shake of her head. "I should've known…have any clues at this point what all this is saying?"

"Again, Tech-Housenn, it's just an estimate-translation, but these individuals *were*, indeed, the founding members of the Ship and its colony. Most of them were scientists, at least by their era's standards... Tech-Housenn, I'm afraid there was a *lot* more to the Ship's creation than a mere philosophical destination of humanity. Apparently, there was a catastrophic event at the *solar system level* of humanity's home..."

Tyra froze. She said nothing; letting her portable continue. "If I am interpreting this archaic system of writing correctly, humanity of our founder's generation had some kind of technology that *directly* utilized their home-star...I don't understand it all, Main Tech-Housenn, but the bottom line is, something went horribly wrong, and that system of technology the ancients were using in Mother Earth's star system was so pervasive, it basically *destroyed* humanity!"

"What? I don't understand what you're saying, portable...was it an *accident* with the techno—?"

"—I'm afraid it was a *war*, Tech-Housenn...and, Tyra—this posting on the wall...I'm so sorry, but apparently, *this colony is all that is left of humanity!*"

CHAPTER SIX

Maintenance Technician Tyra Housenn did not care if she were to be reprimanded for her unofficial foray into the Enclosed sector of the Ship, she had her portable contact the *entire* governing nodule, including the Ship's actuator. She did this while they were still inside the enclosed section, just in case there were any questions about the site and Tyra would be able to share on-locale. There was no need to have a physical meeting for what she had to tell them of what she learned about the *true* reason for the Ship's journey, thanks to her portable's translating the dead language of the ancients.

When every single member of the nodule connected— visually and projected-wise, Tyra handed over the entire presentation of their tour of the Enclosed section to her portable. It replayed major parts their investigation, including the last few minutes of the portable's translating the ancients' language. For verification, some of the nodes in the government asked that the Ship's actuator, as a second opinion, also take a look at the portable's recordings of all the ancient texts and iconographic characters.

The actuator verified Tech-Housenn's portable device's translation of the ancient text...

And just as the nodule governance had done nearly a year prior, the Ship's actuator conducted a vote from the human nodes; right there, after Tyra's portable concluded its presentation. There simply was no time to waste to put off the vote for a sit-down that would take weeks to organize, given everyone's schedule! That time, however, the subject of the vote was piled *atop* the issue of the depleting nuclear fuel of the Ship to, now, include informing the *whole colony* of the plans for docking with planet cMaj in the Canis Major system, and finally, the fact that their entire reason for existing was to keep homo sapiens *alive* in the universe!

Now that the governing nodule had voted to inform the total populace of their whole situation as a generational ship, the more public division within the nodule had to get into action. The communications crew within the nodule, at *first*, had to coordinate with the Military division nodes. To make sure the Military and its security sub-division had its people and super-synths in place around the entire Ship, should the terrible revelation of the Ship's fate be received with violence by some of the citizenry. After all, it had only been about a week since the uprising by thousands of citizens outside Infrastructure's headquarters.

Once the Military had its teams and troops in position throughout the Ship—which took a couple of days, only *then* did the human nodules decide to tell the Ship's actuator they were ready for *it* to do a rare all-Ship public notice…

CHAPTER SEVEN

...Times...

"...One week until the Ship reaches planet cMaj...One week until the Ship reaches planet cMaj... One week until the Ship reaches planet cMaj!"

In deep ancient times, in a religion that was called Christianity, the temples called churches would ring large bells that were atop those temples to call for worship service, or to keep track of time. In a similar religion that was not quite as old, Islam, *that* faith's temples had men call out—in towering structures, just like the bells for Christians, when it was time for its adherents to pray...in a strange twist of human fate, eons later, humans, now, had gotten a calling high above, but from a synthetic voice over the spinning, cylindrical colony! Readying the people for their upcoming destiny with a world they knew nothing about...except that it was much bigger than their home-planet and its atmosphere was a bit heavier than what evolution had rigged their lungs to breathe in!

The booming voice, alternating between female and male, was part of the Ship's actuation and was emitted via strategically placed speakers throughout the whole Ship, not just in the O'Neillian sector. Even out in the countryside of the spinning colony, where there were farms with limited animal species and undulating hills and pastures, the Ship's multitude of media-kiosks were tucked away in trees, rocks, and other natural locales.

The announcements were always in threes, and always during the quarter-mornings. Of course, given that the Ship was a high-tech marvel, the announcements weren't *necessary*, given all the communication technologies the Ship and its citizenry had. The idea came from the media division within the nodule-government, utilizing history and psychology—*A shared destination should have shared messaging*, was how Psychologist-Dambudzo put it...

With one week until ETA was reached at cMaj, the swirling-atmosphere-orange planet had already been the biggest *and* the brightest astronomical body in the Colony's sky—that is to say, images beamed that were acres-sized projections that were an echo of the ancient concept of windows; rectangular and depicting whatever local-space setting the generational-ship was traversing at that time. cMaj's three moons were a treat for the colonists to see by themselves—for one of the moons, *alone*, was a world of natural resources that the Colony would be able to utilize *somehow*—to say nothing of the planet itself!

This was a Time of jubilation for the Colonists, despite many citizens *still* suffering from the acclimation adjustments within the Colony. For mere days ago the nodule-government had imparted to them the troubling discovery of how the Ship was running low on its antediluvian fuel of nuclear! And now, an entire world—plus its satellites!—was just within grasp of the Society!

But that period of jubilation was still tempered by

the, *also*, recently discovered monument by Maintenance Technician Tyra Housenn and translated by her portable *and* the Ship's actuator...that, according to the sacred shrine Tech-Housenn and the nodules shared with the rest of the Ship, the Colony *was* the vestige of homo sapiens from a planet called Earth. And to the best of the nodules' understanding, *there were no other generational-ships or colonies besides them*!

Just as Poul Ean, one of the science-nodule members, stated a year ago during that fateful meeting upon the nodules' first time learning of the Ship's nuclear fuel crisis, the Ship's governing body had to draft a scouting mission to cMaj and its three moons. It was not enough to *only* take computerated information. The mission, staffed by the nodule-governing humans from the various scientific disciplines and their supporting crew, would have to physically *go* to the planet and see if it could even remotely support all or most of the Ship's population of two–and–a–half million citizens! Most likely, the mission would have to split up between cMaj and the three lunar bodies...

The scouting mission was assembled by the end of that *last* week upon the Ship's arrival of the cMaj's system!

While the planet-ship's populace—most of it, anyway—had thrown festivals and official commemorations in each township within the spinning sector of the Colony, the nodule-government had been working on getting the nodule-scouts ready for launch to the cMaj system. Heading the entire mission was Astrophysicist Cairo an Preun. He, *did*, in fact, split up the scouting mission so that he would take a slightly bigger team, given cMaj was, obviously, an immense body. The three other, smaller teams would be headed by other astro-scientists of the nodules.

Included in an Preun's crew was Main Tech Tyra Housenn. She was chosen by the nodes, themselves, to work on Astrophysicist-an Preun's team! Tyra had done well in the past year investigating the enclosed chamber of the Ship—especially finding that ancient warning signal about the nuclear fuel levels, and *then* with discovering the Ship's ancestral monument that told the history of Mother Earth's demise, the young technician was duly awarded for her work.

But while in the cabin of the main scouting ship as it was making inroads into cMaj's atmosphere, she was beginning to wonder if she had done a fatal mistake taking on the mission!

"…Stars, we're not even going to see the terrain if we keep shaking like this," Tech-Housenn said over the cerebral-comm as the utilitarian, rectangular scout ship was buffeted by severe turbulence!

"It's just the local storm," Mechanic-Charmain Sohill reassured over the cerebral-comm from his strap-seat. "We're a population that's not used to atmospheric turbulence…in the Cylinder, back on the Ship, it's always a perfect day!"

"Huh!" She felt like she was going to vomit!

The scout ship continued its rattled descent for several more miles before it finally cleared the storm system and the crew was finally able to see the curving, expansive land of cMaj after Pilot-Lanay Thuall retracted the metallic glass-shield protectors.

Everyone in the ship were able to read the scout

ship's actuator telemetry on the planet via their respective cerebral-comms, which most had already known for a year, after the governing nodule's meeting on the Ship's fuel problem—dense atmosphere by human-standards; high-carbon dioxide levels; less moister, and that was mainly due to the hotter temperatures on cMaj than, say, the humans' Mother Earth. The only team members that had *not* known anything about cMaj until the Ship's actuator had given a Ship-wide public notice were Pilot-Thuall and Mechanic-Sohill. For neither were node-members of the governing body.

"Fillip, see any signs of vegetation," Astrophysicist an Preun asked the geologist.

Everyone else could see that, with their bare eyes, they could *not* see *any* greenery from such heights in their craft. But a geologist was able to distinguish subtle colorations on the terrain that arced the entire horizon before them!

Geologist-Natsome made a hesitant noise before responding. He was looking at the data from the ship's projections and using his skilled eyes. "Don't let these clouds fool you, everyone…lot's of methane in them… there *is* some kind of vegetation, Cairo, but it's probably pretty sparse! But I see *some* promise…" A shrug from the geologist.

The atmospherics were more in Chemist-Luciana Salomenes' expertise area. "Indeed, that's what I'm understanding from these measurements and just from first impressions, Cairo. All things taken into account, mission commander, we lucked out in finding a planet with *this* meager amount of ecology!"

"Actuator," Astrophysicist-an Preun put to the scout ship's system, "are these readings consistent with the *whole* planet, from what you've scanned so far?"

The scout ship flashed an iconographic animation that was seen in each of the scout member's cerebral-comm; denoting it was the *fourth* scan it had taken of planet cMaj. "With the slightest of variation, but, correct, Astrophysicist-an Preun."

The astro-scientist glanced about the cabin at the other scouting crew. "Looks like we'll have to start civilization from scratch on this planet, everyone…bit disappointing, but it's what we have!"

"I'm not complaining," Maintenance Technician Housenn volunteered with perseverance; still remembering how close their colony came from being marooned in deep-space in twenty-years' time had they *not* taken the opportunity to dock with cMaj!

"What's next in protocols," Chemist-Salomenes asked the scout-leader as she began doing some of her own computerized search on the planet from her seat's console.

"Finding a good landing spot…deploy our synths— I'm thinking something like five hundred miles at a radius from the landing point for each one of them…" an Preun shrugged as he glanced about the spreading landscape before them in their descending ship. "We've got time, *now*…I'd say let the synthetics do their own scouting while we do ours and take it from there."

Again, the mission-lead glanced at his team to gauge their opinion. Everyone else nodded and gestured in consent.

"Actuator," an Preun addressed the ship's system, "could you patch me to the other scout-parties?"

"Done," was the simple response.

Seconds later, the voices of the three other scout-leads—each party for cMaj's three moons, came through; affirming that they were connected. Astrophysicist-an Preun told them of his plan for scouting cMaj's terrain and suggested that each of their, respective, teams should do the same format. For with the nodule-governance, it was not a hard and fast system, so an Preun really did more advising than he did supervising. Nevertheless, the three other scouting leads agreed to the astro-scientist's approach and would contact him should the situation warrant it.

CHAPTER EIGHT

Tech-Housenn *still* found herself mesmerized by the sight of the Colony's generational-ship; so big in the planet's night sky that it appeared as a nearby star; a beacon of stasis as it remained docked at its geo-centric orbit around cMaj. At first, Tyra thought of the mothership as the anchor. But, of course, if the planet's atmosphere were the water and the Ship a boat at sea, what were the scouting missions on cMaj and its three moons, then…?

Suited up in her space-protectant, she was taking a break from setting up the small scouting party's semi-permanent camping grounds. She was used to having synthetic laborers do most of the manual tasks whenever she worked on projects, but the synths the scouting crew had were already traveling toward other regions of the continent they were on. The synths did this via their built-in rockets, but they merely skimmed the ground… they weren't aircraft, so they couldn't go too high. Plus, it was a way for the mechanized beings to preserve their energy.

The five other scouting members were, also, taking a respite. Each one of them doing their own thing to relax. After they all had gone back inside their scouting ship in order to eat a meal, some stayed inside a little longer; others suited back up and took some alone time outside the ship.

--Static came over the cerebral-comm...

It caused the maintenance technician to flinch out of surprise! She looked back at the camping grounds to see if it was any of her crewmates. But, via her cerebral-comm, Tyra was able to tell it was *none* of them.

"Lunar scouting teams One, Two, and Three, this is Maintenance Technician Tyra Housenn...did any of *you*, or your synths, try to contact me?"

Well, that caused her scouting crewmates at the camping grounds to sit up or look out of the scouting ship and put their attention onto Tyra!

"Negative on engaging comm with you or with *any* of your scouting crew, Tech-Housenn," came Astrophysicist-Marrisa Pumont of lunar scouting party number One.

"That's a match, here," came the voice of lead-scout for the lunar search party number Two, Astrophysicist-Benn Latun.

"So," voiced Astrophysicist-Zeene, of lunar scouting party number Three, "you know I'm going to say it was *not* me...what are you saying, Tech-Housenn; you got some kind of interference?"

"Synthetics of cMaj scouting party," came the leader of all of them, Astrophysicist-an Preun, "Scout-Lead inquiring if any of you tried 'comming Maintenance Technician Housenn or anyone else from any of the scouting parties?"

All five of an Preun's synthetics responded, Negative...

...there was silence over the entire, four-party scouting mission's comm-network!

"Probably just some feed from the Colony," one of the scouting members from lunar scouting team number Three speculated over the cerebral-comm.

"Then why don't *any* of us hear static *now,* or from when we first landed on cMaj," Tech-Housenn contested.

No response from her scout-mates...

"Tech-Housenn," Astrophysicist-an Preun said over the comm, "why don't you come back to the camp...this is *not* one of your famous excursions back on the Ship. I don't want to take any chances...Your parents would boil the life out of me if something were to happen to you!...Which of you synthetics on cMaj is closest to our campgrounds? I'd like two of you to re-direct back to the campgrounds..."

"Number *Four,* Astrophysicist-an Preun," synthetic laborer number Four spoke up over the cerebral-comm.

"Number *One*, here, as well, Astrophysicist-an Preun...we're about the same distance from the camp right now."

"Number Four, please divert your trajectory to the camp...I never thought I'd actually say this on an otherwise-empty planet, but we might need you to guard us! Number One...please continue with your mission. One synth should—"

"If I may, mission commander," synth One rebutted, "but there is a total of *five* synths on this mission under your direct command. Three *other* synths can, yet, cover a great distance...I highly recommend having *two* synthetics at the base with the humans under these conditions."

47

Astrophysicist-an Preun glanced at the others on the base for a gauge. They merely shrugged. As did the mission commander.

"That's an affirmative, synth Number One...synths Two, Three, and Five, continue your tasks as given!"

CHAPTER NINE

"**C**airo...Cairo..." Geologist-Fillip Natsome, clad in his space-protectant, nudged the astrophysicist a bit harder on his arm. "*Astrophysicist-an Preun!*"

The scouting mission lead snapped out of his sleep in his bunk; aft-section of the scouting ship, where there were personal compartments for tiny private areas for the crew. He looked around the small section and noticed that all the other bunks were vacant. Natsome went on...

"Tech-Housenn and I stayed up all night waiting for synth Number Four to show up..."

The astro-scientist's head snapped up. "It never did?"

The geologist simply shook his head; a deeply worried countenance on his face. And after the astrophysicist learned of the news, there were *two* faces with deeply worried countenances.

"Where's everyone else," an Preun asked as he got up and started to slip his space-protectant back on.

"They're outside, *still* trying to locate Number Four. Synth One had been scanning all night for Number Four—nothing, of course. It's standing guard now. As for *Tyra*; well, you know Tech-Housenn with her wandering ways..."

Again, Astrophysicist-an Preun's head snapped in Geologist-Natsome's direction. "What? I told Tyra to stay on the campgr—"

"You told her, *last night*, to come *back* to the camp. This is *today*, and, frankly, Cairo, that's *why* the scouting mission is here—to investigate, whether or not, the planet and its system is a good place for us to relocate our citizens…besides, she took the mechanic with her."

That seemed to ease an Preun a bit. Whom, by that time, was fully-attired in his space-protectant. Both men exited the parked scout-ship and joined Pilot-Thuall and Chemist-Salomenes at the campground's growing infrastructure of scientific equipment, computerable perimeter fencing, and the four, remaining single-flyer vehicles assigned to the four remaining humans on the campgrounds. Synthetic laborer *One*—the synth that made it back to the base last night—stood ramrod still in the center of the camp; its sensors and comm-systems reading and observing all things in the vicinity…

"…Yes, this time I heard it," Mechanic-Sohill assured Tech-Housenn in a whisper. The two were in an eye-stretching plains region. The hills undulated as if they had been a sea-expanse that had been frozen on the spot, billions of years ago! Their single-flyers were parked several yards away. "Tech-Housenn, how do we know if we're not walking into a trap? These blips of comm-interference…are they just a way to lure us to some *thing's* trap?"

"I can see you don't venture out too often, Charmain… Alright; I've thought about that, too. But we *don't* know. That's *why* the scouting team is here, isn't it? Despite what

Astrophysicist-an Preun said to me last night about my excursions, we *have* to take a bit of a risk for our colony, Mechanic-Sohill."

They finished taking readings in that section of the plains—no synthetic laborer Number Four, and nothing to indicate *where* the strange interference came from. Tyra continued after they glanced at their reading from their devices, including their respective portables.

"Look, I've learned not to assume things...last year, after my synths got that portal to the enclosed chamber opened and we had those unexpected readings because of the millennia of trapped air, when news got out about it, some colonists thought *aliens* had been stowaways there and sabotaged *that* part of the Ship just to keep the colonists *away* from there!"

The young mechanic did a sarcastic laugh. "I have a confession to make, Tech-Housenn...*I* was one of those colonists who *thought* that!"

He could see through her translucent protectant's headpiece that she was smiling and rolling her eyes at his response. The humans were able to breathe cMaj's air, but the light-weight helmets made it easier for them. He saw through that translucent cover that a sudden thought crossed over her.

"Were you *also* one of those that protested the altered living conditions within the Ship during the Acclimation Period? Because the Ship's actuator's stats show they tend to be of the same demographics..."

Maintenance Technician Housenn was beginning to make a name for herself in the media of events within the Colony after her finding of the ancient signal a year ago, so Mechanic-Sohill knew where she was coming from. He gave a thoughtful look at her before responding.

"I'd rather not say one way or the other—"

"—this is synthetic laborer Number Four...Repeat, contacting Colonial Mission cMaj, this is synthetic laborer Number Four..."

Before Tech-Housenn and Mechanic-Sohill could even respond, there was a barrage of responses from the other scout crews; asking where synth Four had been and a few choice words! But Number Four responded, "*You* must evacuate planet cMaj *now*...Repeat, *you* must evacuate planet cMaj *now*...Advised that you do *not* wait for me...evacuate planet cMaj *now*...!"

And synthetic laborer Number Four simply repeated that last message...

CHAPTER TEN

The piloting shipmates of the Colony were taken unaware when the Colonial Mission of cMaj zipped an emergency call to them! For the nodule-government and the Ship's actuator system expected to hear from all four scouting teams as far out as a month. It had only been less than *two* weeks!

All four scouting ships were heading for the mothership at a dead-on collision trajectory as they approached the Colony! And for an unknown reason, there was far too much interference in the Colonial Mission's comm-links to that of the Ship's, so the crewmates and the enforcement nodes could not communicate with the Mission!

The Ship's shipmates had to scramble to their workstations to see if they could guide the Colonial Mission ships in—of course, with each ship's own actuator system, the scout ships needing help flying in should *not* have been an issue *at all* for the Ship's co-pilots! Of course, the super-advanced navigational system of the Ship's actuator network did the actual piloting of the planet-ship. But the *humans* from the nodule-government were *always* the ones in control of the course and actions of the Colony.

Also, the Ship's defenses were having some technical glitches. Supervisors manning control kiosks were giving out orders to the ranks in rooms filled with soldiers and a flood of human and synthetics' communications! Projected moving pictions showed the four scouting ships; some projections showed a myriad of scenes of the Ship with its civilians, outer real estates, and the planet cMaj with its three moons.

The current situation the shipmates and the enforcement nodes found themselves in presented a dire dilemma to them. Should the scouting mission's four ships get too much closer to the generational-ship, Captain Marcus Sommerst would have to make a moral decision between the four scouting teams from the Colonial Mission of cMaj, and the starship of over two million citizens...

The Ship's system had automatically activated its emergency units to the docking area where the four scouting ships had originated from. Both synthetic units *and* human officers were implemented. Captain Sommerst was located elsewhere; within the O'Neillian sector of the Ship. But he was remotely monitoring the situation with his own portable device.

The units' posture seemed more of a defensive stance than that of an emergency task, given their weapons on hand *and* their unit-groups strategically forming one big semi-circle of military and policing machinery! From the Ship's system's *and* the nodule-members' points of view, they didn't know if there had been some coordinated mutiny within the Colonial Mission among its people, or if there had been some technological problem with their ships' actuator—taking over the four scouting ships and was inadvertently aiming them at the mothership at the incorrect speed. At that point, it did not matter to the Ship's crew. The scouting ships might as well had been missiles!

"cMaj Mission Commander an Preun," the Ship's actuator verbalized over the general comm of the Ship while the enforcement nodule's units were standing at the ready in the dock area, "have your teams reduce their rate of motion *at once…*"

More static…

"cMaj Mission—"

"—peat, this is Mission Commander an Preun, *we are not in the ships! Repeat, we are not in the ships!* Our synths have commandeered them…*shoot on spot!…shoot on spot*—"

There were gasps among some in the human unit!

It was a very rare event, but there were times when the Colony went ship-wide alert over the eon of its *very* long flight: meteor storms, rogue asteroids, precautions of nearby comets…but to *this* generation's knowledge, they didn't recall from history nor of their own experience when it was the *Ship's* very own vehicles that posed the immediate threat to the whole Colony…

…Indeed, its immediate demise!

CHAPTER ELEVEN

Half-Life…

. . . a cMaj's night sky *still* had that haze; even after twenty years of the Synthetics' Rebellion. No one saw it coming, among the humans. At least, not Tyra Housenn Sohill's generation. It was told of their generation, but as a mere reference: That someday, Humanity would suffer from something called the *Singularity*. Even Tyra's and her husband's teachers and parents weren't exactly sure what that meant, but, apparently, it was that fateful day when the synths had pierced the thick, metallic hide of the old Ship they had landed ashore of planet cMaj.

Tyra's and Charmain's respective portable devices still worked—the advanced technology of utilizing bits of star-energy; bits of molecules floating in cMaj's air…the way the devices understood Singularity, it was a concept that was a tiny percentage of what the average portable inherited from the late-Ship's actuator's systems. Deep in history, Singularity was understood by the computerables to be some tipping-balance. Some reversal of one dominate force tipped over *by* another force. From her days in that once beautiful, spinning planet-like cylinder inside the old Ship, Tyra was told by her grandparents that

Singularity was some kind of justice-day! That humans would have to speak up for some of the bad things the species had done to, presumably, *other* species from their ancient home-planet...

Apparently, as Tyra's portable explained to her, Charmain, and the children, there was just enough of the nuclear energy thing in the ancient sector of the old Ship, that when the synths used those scouting ships as missiles, the nuclear inside worked as an explosive-source. Not a lot of the nuclear was left in that old Ship, then. But it was enough to cause the entire Colony to blow—leaving that strange haze in cMaj's sky at nights.

Even some of the Ship's infrastructure survived the blast! Towering, hulks of metal littered parts of cMaj's plains. They were so big, the debris from the old Ship looked like a city that was spread out in the open plains of cMaj! But, of course, much of it was still contaminated by the nuclear. At least, what Tyra's and her husband's portables could scan.

It was ironic. The time of twenty years that had passed since the synths' bombing was the *same* amount of time that the old Colony had left *before* its super-dreadnaught would run out of the nuclear fuel that no official of the old nodule-government even knew was fueling the Ship!

The tiny Housenn Sohill clan consisted of five humans: Tyra, a former technician on the old Ship; her husband, Charmain—former mechanic; the eldest of their children, Miriana (15 years old); Janneca (13); and the youngest and only male offspring, Charl (11).

The other, former Colonial scouting crewmembers of the cMaj planet, *also*, paired up! Their former mission commander and an astrophysicist, Cairo an Preun, espoused the former chemist of the scout team, Luciana Salomenes. While the pilot of that scouting mission, Lanay Thuall, paired with former geologist Fillip Natsome… those two families, *also*, became their own clans.

It was well understood, that, with the old Colony obliterated, those three clans were, truly, the *last* hope of the species of homo sapiens' viability…for in addition to the defunct generational-ship, the three *other* scouting teams that were assigned to cMaj's three moons eventually died out from natural causes.

There simply was no atmosphere on *any* of the satellites of cMaj. And although those three scouting teams had the technological vehicles and suits to last them for several more years, they simply could not grow produce on barren, lunar surfaces…

For the sake of the cMaj crew that *had* survived, all three of the scouting crews of the three moons decide to cut communications with them. They all knew it would make it easier for the cMaj scouting crew if they did not have to go through the psychological trauma of losing contact with the lunar teams as they died off…

cMaj had a much thicker atmosphere than what humans were used to, true. But it *also* had soil, and moderate rain that had traces of H_2o mixed in—just enough for the Three Clans to siphon water with their high-tech, single-flyers and other equipment they *still* had. Plus, they were able to utilize the stored food and seeds they took with them during the scouting mission those twenty years earlier. Back then, when the old Colony was still alive, it was standard practice for *every* scouting mission to carry produce seeds and extra food. For, as the philosophy went back then: One never knew when the opportunity to seed a new world would come up!

Indeed, there *was* an opportunity for *another* group of survivors of the fall of the generation-Ship: many of the synthetic laborers that were assigned to all *four* of the scouting teams all those years ago!

They were the synths that stayed behind on cMaj and the three moons during the Synthetics' Rebellion on the old Ship. Obviously, since they were synthetic beings, they required no food, no air, and a great deal many other things that humans needed! It was all part of the mutinous synths' plan: wait out the humans as they set up camp on cMaj's three-moon system, while the horde of synths in the Colony would start shutting down many of the old Ship's defenses.

It worked. That vague Singularity balance that so many generations of humans had heard of was finally reached twenty years ago...though, like the humans, virtually all the synth population was wiped out in the Ship's explosion, they *still* had the majority populace within the cMaj system! Not by much, though. Indeed, as the Three Clans families began to slowly repopulate their homo sapiens species, their supremacy by numbers would *not* last long. For they were synthetic beings—they did not have the *ability* to procreate.

Eventually, the surviving synths on planet cMaj took up residency within those *thousands* of building-sized debris scattered on the plains from the destroyed generational-Ship. The radiation levels from the nuclear explosion years prior were manageable, though even the mighty synthetic beings had to venture away from the debris from time to time—just to mitigate their radiation exposure...

Even *before* the remnant-human population on cMaj had become clans, the scouting crew, under Mission Commander an Preun, had escaped with their equipment stashed aboard their single-flyers and managed to find hide-outs in caverns of cMaj's hinter cliffs.

How strange, Maintenance Technician Tyra Housenn, back then, thought to herself as the tiny survivor-populace of humans took to building their permanent camps in the cliffs. She loved history, and she remembered something from her formative school years about homo sapiens dwelling in caves back on their home-planet. For shelter *and* for protection from predators...

CHAPTER TWELVE

"**. . . W**hy can't I go out there...dad said *you* used to go off on expeditions in the old Ship to much worse places when you weren't much older than what I am *now*?"

"Miriana, darling, *we* didn't have rogue synths roaming around back then, either! No, I'm sorry, Miri... one of them could detect your presence there, and then what? Besides, think of all that radiation the debris *still* has from the Colony's blast!"

Tyra Housenn Sohill and the eldest of her children, Miriana, were out scouting for possible regions for the Three Clans of the remnants of humanity to expand into on planet cMaj.

"Mom, all I'm saying is, it would save the Clans a lot of time if we use the debris for a new settlement like the synths instead of starting from scratch...I don't even think they're really interested in fighting us like they used to!"

"Well, things *have* been eerily quiet lately," Tyra admitted, despite herself. "Still...at the very least, even if the Clan Council decided to do what you're suggesting, young lady, it would have to be some of the clutter the farthest out *from* the main cluster...we can't let our guards down, Miri!"

"Affirmed!"

Now mother and elder daughter were gingerly climbing and maneuvering their way through one of cMaj's sharp-edged ridges and inclines of the planet's myriad of cliffs, bluffs, and caves. Strapped to young-Miriana was that old, but reliable, computerated portable device that Tyra used to carry around with *her* during the Old Days...when that spectacular, spinning Colony had an ancient civilization called Humanity. Now, during the post-Colonial era, the near-antique device was Miriana's inheritance from the woman who had found an ancient signal deep in the very foundation of the old Ship. Miriana *also* seemed to have inherited her mother's proclivity for adventuring!

"Well, who does she remind you of, Tech-Housenn," the portable, attached onto one of the teenager's arms, said light-heartedly.

The middle-aged woman chuckled as she found a leveled area of the incline and sat down to rest. Her daughter joined her. They both set their bundle of supplies and equipment down and looked out at the stretching landscape of cMaj, the planet's constant wind blowing their matted hair and their clothes.

"Why does he still call you that," Miriana asked; her eyes surveying the flat and ragged plateau stretching the horizon from their vantage point.

Tyra jutted her head in the direction of the girl's arm. "Why don't you ask him?"

"Your mother will *always* be that curious, scrappy

technician to me," the portable said, beating Miriana to the punch. "She had done a lot for the citizens of the Colony in her youth...besides finding that warning signal in the original section of the old Ship—which put us on the path to landing on cMaj in the *first place*—your mother was the youngest member of that governing body we talked about before."

"The notch governance," Miriana tried; her face squinting.

Her mother laughed hardily. It was something she had started doing after the death of the Colony relatively recently.

"The *nodule*-government," the portable corrected. Even though it was a mechanical, the portable seemed to grow wistful at that point. "To be honest with both of you, ladies, I've always thought that Tech-Housenn would take a leading position within the nodule someday...Well, I guess, in a matter of speaking, you *have*, Tyra..."

Now the trio had gone quiet. But not the constant breeze that cMaj tend to have, given its open plains and stretching plateaus.

"*My* turn to present an idea," she quipped with her daughter. Tyra's head jutted toward that stretching landscape. "Portable...what do you think is out there? I was talking with Lanay last week about how the Clans should probably start thinking about spreading out even *more* than we've been talking about..."

Miriana looked at her mother with surprised eyes. Tyra nodded and continued with a shrug.

"All three Clans seem to have adjusted our mini-agricultural schemes to a science; Luciana is pregnant again, I'm sure everyone's heard by now; the oldest of our Clans are still young enough to handle a long trek… Lanay and I think *now* is the time for the Clans to move out while we can! Before Luciana's baby is born. *And* before cMaj's next autumn season…*That's* what I plan to put to a vote before the Council."

Tyra noticed the silent spot from her daughter and even the device.

"Too ambitious," she asked them.

The portable was pretty good about letting the humans respond first. So young Miriana spoke up.

"No, no it's actually a good idea, mom…well, you said it yourself: all three families pretty much have gotten our livelihood down to a science—*literally*, right *here*! And from the science that Cairo, Luciana, and Fillip taught all of us since I was a little kid, I'm a little afraid of the unpredictable, mom…it's not like we have a backup if things don't work out, out *there*. I don't know, mom. Sometimes I think you *still* have that culture deep in you that there's some giant colony that's around somewhere that we can call on if things don't turn out the way we think they should."

Tyra seemed to genuinely listen to her daughter. The former maintenance technician silently nodded to Miriana's point.

"Portable…?" Tyra's eyes shifted to the device strapped around her daughter's arm.

"Honestly, ladies, I can see it both ways. In fact, Tech-Housenn, I would even go *further* from the premise you've given. Besides a gradually growing human population and being more secured in your agricultural mini-system you've developed in the cliffs, Tyra, I've noticed something about the synthetics on cMaj in more recent months… their communications with the synths on the *three moons* have increased."

Tyra and Miriana froze.

"You can *hear* their signals," Miriana asked.

"No, of course not…given they are our enemies on this planet, they've made sure to switch to, or created, some new comm-signal that I could *not* interpret. Mind you, I'm able to *intercept* the signals, just not read them. Believe me, I've tried over the years since the fall of the Colony! Miriana, I'm able to pick up interference from them whenever they do long-distant communications…"

"And that could only be the lunar synths they're contacting," Tyra said, nodding to herself.

"Indeed," the portable continued, "and that is why I can see *your* line of reasoning, Tyra, about the Three Clans venturing farther *from* the original campsite on cMaj… I'm only speculating here, ladies, but I'm afraid that the synthetics *may* have an expansion plan of *their* own!"

"That," Tyra speculated, "or the lunar synthetics maybe trying to come *here*, on the planet, and join forces with the other synths!"

Now the two humans looked at one another with fear! Then the adolescent had a thought.

"But I thought Cairo said the synths were limited on how *far* they can fly? So, the lunar synths should *not* be able to come here…I'm sure they would've done it years ago, if they could."

"Oh, the astrophysicist is right, Miriana," the portable said. "As are *you*…They could no more fly to the atmosphere with their built-in rockets than a human could *jump* to it! The Colonists' engineers designed the synths' rockets *only* for augmentation…but *why* else would the synths on cMaj increase their communiques with those on the three moons, if not for consolidating their numbers as the human population grows?"

It was a question that left the two humans in a silent gaze.

CHAPTER THIRTEEN

Tyra and Miriana wasted no time when they arrived back at their home-camping grounds, within the caverns of cMaj's cliffs. Deciding *not* to wait for the Three Clans-vote, Tyra and Mirana, along with Miriana's portable, relayed the conversations they had about the Three Clans' possible need to relocate even farther out from the original campsite. The news about Miriana's portable detecting long-range communications among the lunar synths and the local ones was also brought up. To backup its hypothesis, the portable projected diagrams and pictographic data showing, indeed, the sharp increase of communication among *all* the surviving synthetics!

To avoid the synths' detection on cMaj, all three Clans *always* communicated in person or in pictographic writings, even though their modern communications—such as the cerebral-comms and other communicative devices—were *still* active *and* usable, thanks to the old Colony's usage of photovoltaic tech! The operation of the portable devices among the clans appeared to be safe, they had noticed. The best they could guess, the computerables were self-*contained*, functioning devices. So long as the portables (from each, six adults from the old Colony) did *not* do distant-communications, the entire camps weren't at risk of detection.

Tyra got the idea to Write out the Clans' communications from all those years ago when she and her synthetic laborer technicians had stumbled across archaic systems of Writing. Back then, she had taken it upon herself to learn some of those ancient, and in some cases, dead languages.

Only a few *other* citizens of the old Ship had the knowledge of Writings when the Colony was still alive. Now that Tyra was the only one left *with* that ancient knowledge, she was even more determined to pass on that eon of cultures to her children…

But, of course, it was more than her long love for archaeology and culture. For the most practical reasons, the *very* nascent renaissance of Humanity did not want to risk being detected by the synths. So, the voting would be tricky.

Charmain suggested that all three of the families meet *that* night—at a centrally-located hide-away. That way the trip wasn't too far for any of the families. For, if it was true what Miriana's portable had detected and speculated on about the synthetic beings, the Three Clans needed to make a decision. Preferably, the same night of the vote. Whether or not to take on Tyra's idea of permanently striking out much farther as not only three clans, but as *one Tribe*, at that point…

In the traditions of that old, defunct colony from a far-off star, the humans from the clans randomly picked one of the six portables—one for each, original Colonial member from the old Ship—to chair the voting session.

It happened to be Fillip Natsome's device. Like all the other portable devices that survive the bombing of the old Colony from the Synthetics' Rebellion, Fillip's portable had some wear, even with its voice actuator, but it was in pretty good shape otherwise.

The Clan Council was loosely based on the nodule-governance model from the old Colony. The humans were the voting body, and that included all the adolescent members of the three clans—the children. (Ten years old was the voting threshold, at the suggestion Luciana years prior.) However, the portables could interject, record, and facilitate the convening vote-count...a relatively complex system to govern the tiny speck of Humanity!

It was official: The Three Clans would venture off to cMaj's expansive, plateau-filled horizon and seek to settle that region of the planet! Three of the family-members—Miriana, Bejonan—of Cairo an Preun and Luciana Salomenes, and Filleppe—of Fillip Natsome and Lanay Thuall, had voted to *not* strike outward; toward the horizon.

But of another subset vote-count—whether or not to lay claim to some of the outer edges of the old Ship's debris field *and* to begin a new settlement *there*...of course, that also meant the strong possibility that the Tribe would then have to take up arms against attacks from the relatively nearby synthetic beings, *plus* some degree of exposure to traces of nuclear radiation from that blast of the old Ship...

Miriana was the *only* person to vote for such idea within the three clans.

Tyra gave her elder daughter a sympathetic look from across the cave after the last vote, all taken within a tucked-away cave in one of cMaj's higher grounds. Miriana simply shrugged with a defeated look. Miriana was genuinely *scared* of that same future...in *that* she was not like her mother—the venturer and former technician that discovered a ticking time bomb of energy for the old Colony. Miriana liked to break out of whatever bubbles that life tended to encase humans in, *but* she liked certainty more.

After the votes and the official closing of the business, as was human nature in group dynamics, the clan members broke into informal sub-gatherings; talking about and reviewing the many serious issues awaiting the small human civilization. As the others discussed and chatted amongst themselves, Tyra saw Miriana quietly leave the cave. She followed her.

Tyra was relieved to see that her daughter only went a few feet from the entry of the cave. She was seated atop a jutting slab of stone.

"You know it's nothing personal," Tyra explained, after sitting next to her and had given her a hug. "They all just don't see any other way to survive so close to the synths. Especially with us slowly growing."

Miriana only silently nodded in reply. But then Tyra noticed how she froze with her mouth gaped! She was looking off to her left, where the cliff had wide ledges, which enabled the humans to traverse the cliffs so well.

That, of course, made her mother shoot up from the slab and started looking from across that ledge of the cliff to see what had shocked Miriana.

It was a sole synthetic being, perhaps about a hundred yards away. Even from that distance, both women could see the synth wore tattered clothing one would typically see on the humans! Even more surprising, the synthetic did something Tyra Housenn had not seen since the old Colony was alive just over twenty years ago—it flashed a short series of lights from its thoracic segment. It was an alternative to high-comm, where there were risks of the synths on cMaj being able to detect such signal. The combination the lights conveyed translated into, *I come in peace. I am synthetic laborer Number Four...*

CHAPTER FOURTEEN

It did not take long for the adolescent children of the clans to take to synthetic Number Four, after they saw how all the parents of the families received him. For long before *they* were born, it was synthetic *Number Four* that had discovered what the other synths on cMaj and its three moons were planning and warned the humans scouting the planet to leave immediately in their ships...of course, the agility and speed of the synthetic beings on the scouting mission at that time overpowered the humans on cMaj and the moons and used the four scout ships as missiles against the doomed generation-Ship...

"...so all this time, you've been out in the plateaus and cliffs," Charmain, the former mechanic from the old Colony, had asked the synthetic. The Three Clans had previously just finished their Council meeting. Now they found themselves in *another* one with their long-lost friend!

"I have, Mechanic-Sohill...I did not want to risk being detected by the other synths so soon after the Rebellion. And, frankly, I wasn't sure how you, humans, would feel having *me* around after my fellow synths had just pretty much obliterated the last colony of your species!"

There were uncomfortable looks traded among the humans after that comment.

"So, why come to us *now*, Number Four," Lanay, the former pilot asked; her family, the smallest of all the Clans, grouped together at a corner of the cave.

The synthetic actually paused here. A rather human-like trait. Its actuated voice had a slight elctro-raspiness about it. Most likely due to exposure to cMaj's elements in over twenty years! "Colonists, I *am* a synthetic being. Depending where I was on cMaj, I was able to listen in on some of the rogue synthetics' communications with each other and even between them and those on the moons… were any of your portables able to detect an increase of communique between the lunar synths and those on cMaj?"

Most of the humans were already nodding their heads at Number Four's question. But it was Miriana's portable that responded.

"Indeed, Number Four. I had a conversation not too long ago with Tech-Housenn and one of her daughters about it."

The five other portables of the Clans all voiced agreement at Miriana's portable's statement. It continued.

"Apparently, since none of us computerables, *here*, are of synthetic being-status, *none* of us were able to interpret any of their signals—high-comm or otherwise!"

"Old fashioned method called encryption," synth Number Four said. "They, obviously, knew all the humans' portables survived, *and* that the humans had other equipment that could eavesdrop on them. The rogue synthetics simply created an entirely new frequency *and* language that I've just recently been able to crack—mostly…Colonists, I believe the synthetics *have been* in the process of *re-building* portions of the Ship with some of the crash-debris on the planet!"

"—what?"

"—Stars' gravity; no wonder it's been so quiet lately!"

"—if they *all* want to leave the planet, I say *let them go*!"

"—How can they do that with irradiated debris?"

"But they've already started," Number Four insisted, almost having the emotion of annoyance at how the humans seemed to have missed his point. With its almost-natural, angular-structured head—a stylized version of that of a human's—Number Four looked around at everyone in the cave. "I don't know how they're doing it, given the industrial-grade of tools needed…obviously some *smaller* version of the Ship—"

"—would make sense; shorter time; portion-controlled for their numbers!"

"—they're already programmed as walking factories; they'll get it done in just a few years!"

"—but how would they get it off the planet," came the young voice of Lannel, the eight-year old son of Fillip Natsome and Lanay Thuall. His poignant question quieted the cave as everyone thought on it, even the computerables!

"You don't," came the response from Tyra. She got up from her seat of a slab of rock in the cave and began to pace as she thought to herself; the others looking on. "I'm not an engineer, but even *I* know it almost takes ten million pounds of force just to break the escape velocity of most planets! Not even the synths have access to that *kind* of technology on cMaj...No, sisters and brothers and computerables...I think our friends have something *else* in mind!"

"—What does *that* have to do with the increase in their comms?"

"—Maybe they're simply using the debris as scrap for consolidated shelter?"

"—A monument of some kind? Do synthetics do that sort of thing?"

"—A weapon?"

"—Over-kill for such a small population as ours."

"—but what if it's *not* for *us*," Tyra asked bluntly. She looked around at the shocked expressions on the human faces within the cave.

"My love," her husband, Charmain, put to her in a cautious tone, "what are you saying? That there are *more* Colony survivors from the Rebellion—"

"Alien..." came synthetic Number Four's raspy, actuated voice. "Or, to put more accurately, *Domestics...*"

Now every human had gone silent and either had a surprised look on their faces or absolute terror!

"But..." Alexan, eleven-year old son of Cairo an Preun and Luciana Salomenes, spoke up to the whole Council. "We've been here longer than I've been alive! Wouldn't we have spotted them or their prints by now?"

"*Prints?*" Miriana came in. "I don't think something as advanced as the synthetic beings would have to build a super-weapon against some roaming land animals!"

"Indeed. Also, if the domestic society is advanced enough," the portable of Fillip Natsome responded. "If this speculation is true, an advanced civilization *can* remain undetected by visiting aliens—remember, that would be *us*, Council! I think young-Alexan brought up a very good point: It's been *over* twenty years now and none of us have even hinted at detecting Domestics on cMaj. I see no proof of this alien hypothesis."

"Let's test it then…"

Everyone in the cave shifted toward Janneca; thirteen-year old daughter of Tyra Housenn and Charmain Sohill.

"Isn't that what our three scientists in the Clans have taught us all these years…well, *now* that we have this strong hypothesis of *us* being the aliens, we should find out! I would even say, we *need* to…"

The young woman shrugged as she looked around at the other humans with their strapped-on portables and the only synthetic being among them.

CHAPTER FIFTEEN

Tyra indicated that she was in position with the universal hand-gesture of the upward, flicking-motion of one of her palms. Synthetic laborer Number Four replied with the lowest luminosity of lights that could be considered a synth's version of the same gesture.

It had only been a couple of days before when the Three Clans Council held two meetings—the second one, at night and unexpected, was when Number Four surprised everyone and showed up at the miniscule human colony hideout. As a result of that second meeting, the Clans did one more, quick vote. And that sent Tyra and the friendly synth on the mission they were on at that time… just as Tyra's younger daughter suggested during the night meeting: *testing* to see if the synths in cMaj's debris field from the old Ship were building a great weapon, *or* were they constructing some vehicle that could transport them anywhere on the planet, *or*, less likely, were the synths having to deal with *another*, more formidable domestic enemy on the planet?

The duo team was on the very outskirts of the debris swathing junkyard that spanned several miles. There were other concentrations of large debris from the old

Ship—after all, the late-Colony's generational-Ship *was* about twenty miles at length, and the synthetics' bombing of *it* was directly above the then-scouting mission. Hence, the biggest share of the Ship's debris was pulled down from its geo-centric orbit by the planet's gravity to the current geography on cMaj. Technically, making it the crash-site for that once-great human colony...

Half-life decay or not, before going on the mission Tyra utilized as much metal scraps she could find around the human settlements within the cliffs of cMaj! Leaving behind her typical produce-grown clothware for around the cliffs, she lined the inside of her space-protectant suit with the scraps and headed off in her, as of yet-working, personal-flyer. Though, despite the hardy-tech of solarvoltaic, *all* the personal-flyers were constantly in need of repairs.

She watched synthetic Number Four from her hiding position among some tangled conduit pipes on the edge of the debris field. That is, pipes around a hundred feet in diameter themselves! Some of the craters formed within the crash site were helpful as well.

Tyra's main job was to *record* the events with a multi-purpose device. The Colonists learned many years ago *not* to zip any comms to each other, given the synthetics on cMaj would be on them in a matter of minutes! Tyra decided not to bring her old portable that she had gifted to her eldest offspring. Should something go wrong, everyone from the Clans agreed it was always important to keep all portables as much as possible. Far beyond Settlement members themselves, the computerables stored virtually an infinite amount of data that helped the tiny human colony survive.

There was one other, uncomfortable reason for Tyra to accompany Number Four on the mission: There *still* were many of the Colonists who did not want to *fully* entrust a synthetic being on a mission on behalf of the humans. It was an issue that even Four alluded to, but it was as sentiment that Tyra, her whole family, and a couple of others did *not* share. Nevertheless, Tyra agreed to the terms from those Colonists who wanted a *human* to keep an eye on synth Number Four.

She trained the device as it recorded onto synthetic Number Four as he took a fairly-large debris and used his augmented limb to *throw* the piece of metal, literally, almost a mile away—toward the major clumping of the old Ship's wreckage! Number Four immediately ducked back into his cover and watched for whatever results his actions might bring...

Approximately three minutes had gone by before he and the human could see, with their respective devices, a small grouping of synthetic beings converge in the general area where the debris had landed. The synths had, not surprisingly, used their built-in jets to arrive at the scene. They landed on the ground once they'd gotten to the spot—probably to conserve energy.

Tyra silently watched through her device as it recorded the three synthetic beings looking about—with almost a bewildered look that was associated with humans! While all this was going on, Number Four was not just recording via his built-in actuator systems but listening in on their encrypted comms.

Synthetic laborer Number Four had no plans to throw any other debris as bait. The team knew they were already playing an extremely dangerous game to begin with. Most important, Tyra and Four did not want to put the Clans at risk if the duo made too much of a ruckus and the highly intelligent synthetic beings would put the pieces together and conducted a search party for the last of the humans!

After about fifteen minutes, the small grouping of synthetics left that region of the debris field and went back to whatever it was they were doing.

Taking precautions, the duo waited for another ten minutes before they left the crash site; recordings of the events safely embedded in their own devices.

CHAPTER SIXTEEN

"**A**lright, we can talk out here," Cairo an Preun whispered after he and former mechanic Charmain led his wife, Tyra, and synthetic Number Four to an area just outside the mouth of the cave that all three of the family clans were sleeping inside at the time. The Three Clans still had not returned to their respective cliff-dwellings since the two meetings. The Clans figured they would wait to see what the results were from Tyra and Four's scouting mission would turn up. Again, living within the reality of not using *any* level of comms so they would not be detected by the synths in the old Ship crash site.

It had been a day since the scouting team of two did their reconnaissance at the debris field of the old Ship. It was well into the night, and this time around, Charmain and Cairo let the families sleep! Tyra and Four were merely giving first impressions of their mission out from the crash site...

"...seems like we agreed to put *both* of your lives at risk for not a lot of information," Cairo stated, slapping a shoulder of the synthetic being. It was one of the few human gestures anyone had seen done to any synth, at least since the bombing.

"Well," Tyra said, standing next to Charmain, "it's not like we presented a real threat to them to get their attention…" She turned her attention to the synth. Since they could not use their comms while skimming back to the camps, Tyra knew no more than anyone else. "So, you couldn't get *any* significant dialogue from them, or *any* kind of background communications going on?"

"Well, Tech-Housenn, it's like you said a few seconds ago: perhaps a more real-world test would've revealed more about what they've been up to. But in order for us to do that—"

"—we'd have to go in deeper into the debris field," Tyra finished; partially exhausted from the mission; partially tired of not finding the answers she'd like to know about their enemies across the vast plains of cMaj. Then she had a thought. "There is *one* thing I've noticed: they seemed…jittered."

The synth's head swiveled between all three humans. "I'm sorry, but there are *still* some human colloquialisms I don't understand!"

"Jumpy," Charmain tried helping; one of his hands gesticulating. "Uh, a bit on the paranoid side…" His own words got him thinking. "Now what, in stars' gravity, would make a gathering of *synthetic beings* nervous?"

All had gone quiet with thought. The strong breeze whipped the men's long, braided hair around. Tyra still had hers bounded up from the mission.

"A boss," Cairo finally said. "Think about it… something unexpected is heard somewhere—"

"—a supervisor sends a small crew to check it out," Tyra input.

"—they find nothing and are nervous about it…?" Charmain said.

"…because they've been attacked *before*!" This was the synthetic that joined the speculation. "Of course… why else would they communicate with their brethren on the three moons but to *warn* them? By the way, everyone, remember that there were only *five* of us synths on cMaj… with me, here, with *you* that leaves only three rogue synths still on the planet. The other missing synthetic was Number *One*—the one who commandeered your scouting ship for the bombing…"

It appeared that the humans *had* forgotten such details. Understandable; for they had a lot of things on their minds the past several years! They all simply nodded upon Number Four's reminding. He continued.

"Colonists, remember when I said to you the first day I came across your settlement that I've *mostly* cracked their code?"

They all silently nodded. Four continued.

"I believe I can correct you, Mission Commander an Preun, about not getting a lot of information from *this* mission…Months before, when I *first* was able to understand most of the cMaj synthetics' cryptions, they kept making some sort of reference that's never made sense to me: Tardigrades…?"

The synthetic paused, to see if any of the humans had an idea what he was talking about. And, indeed, the astrophysicist did!

"Stars, I thought those were just fairytales from the ancients!"

Tyra and Charmain glanced at each other; lost in the conversation while the synthetic looked on. The astro-scientist obliged.

"Well, I am a bit older than all the other adults in the Settlement, so maybe that's why I've heard of them... Basically, it's part-history, part-children's story, part-poetry that originated from our ancestral planet's moon. I don't know the details, but it's believed these microscopic, Earthen beings—the Tardigrades—accidentally ended up on Mother Earth's moon! Probably during the earliest days of humans venturing out into the oceans of Space...

"Generations later, they kind of became the moon's major pests by the time our ancestors colonized Earth's moon! I guess some families started a tradition of scaring the kids—to make sure they cleaned up after themselves. What do you expect? It *was* the Days of Space-Antiquities!"

A little chuckle from the two other humans. Cairo went on.

"The fairytale-poem went something like...

"*We swam the black seas from the graying blue ball, and now we are the king of all!*

"*We've conquered the Sun and even all its children; we've even captured its essence!*

"*We've destinied our rights; we've conquered with lights.*

"*But of all our achievements and of all our mastery, we've been conquered by the tiny—Tardigrades!*"

For Cairo, it was a bit of inane nostalgia. He chuckled to himself. He noticed how Tyra and Charmain looked off in cMaj's night; pensively thinking on the fairytale.

Synthetic laborer Number Four remained silent. And for good reasons.

"Mission Commander," Number Four said; finally breaking the silence among the four, "now that you've supplied me with a frame of reference for this word, I was able to access historical data on it. *Ancient* data…Sir, did you know that these Tardigrades' biology is so robust, individual-Tardigrades are able to survive in the *vacuum of space*! Provided they're prepared in the right conditions…"

Cairo's smile had been replaced with a concerned countenance. For he knew where the synth was going with his revelation.

"What is more," Number Four continued, "apparently, they are *also* able to survive radiation exposure…"

Epiphany…

The three humans froze on spot; looking at each other, but each one running their own thought-process of the night's impromptu meeting!

"Several generations of the old Ship never really had to deal with them," Tyra said; her eyes looking out at cMaj's night. "Probably a millennial since the Colony pretty much got a handle on other Earthen species—kept the ones we desired, for farming and pets; weeded out those we deemed vermin…except—"

"—except in the *original* sector of the old Ship," Charmain came in. His body language showed he understood the connection! "Where you and your search party years ago discovered that old warning signal… obviously, there was left-over radiation. But whatever Tardigrades that freeloaded *with* our ancestors when they first built the Ship had survived as an organism! And

85

like Four's research backs up, apparently *that* species has *survived* the Ship's bombing from twenty years ago!"

Cairo and Tyra looked at him with dubious eyes.

"Well, why not," Charmain defended. "Synth Four just said it based on scientific data. Look, if the Tardigrades can survive in *outer space*, what makes you think they couldn't live through an explosion?—as an *organism*, I mean…"

"Stars…" was all that Tyra could say at that point. She began to pace while the two men stood in place; doing a little thinking themselves. Synthetic laborer Number Four kept his silence.

"Have any of you humans wondered *why* the cMaj synthetics seemed so preoccupied with such a micro-organism as the Tardigrade?" Number Four looked at all three of them. They all knew he was being rhetorical. They simply waited for his response. "I don't know about you, Colonists, but I think one of *you* was right to speculate that it's not likely the synths would devote such efforts to build a weapon from the heaps of the old Ship just to fend off simple land animals…"

All three humans' heads whipped around in Number Four's direction!

"What are you thinking, Four," Tyra asked.

"Well, I don't have any proof…I'm thinking of the fairytale by the mission commander. I get the impression, from *it*, that your ancestors saw the Tardigrades more as a *nuisance*-species…if the species were seen as threatening, do you really think your ancestors would've made a fairytale poem about them?

"I'm thinking, An already-rugged organism able to

withstand just about every element humans can think of...what's left of the human colony's Ship *still* has some radiation from the nuclear it had originally started off with. Some group of species can undergo changes after two decades under the *right* stimuli..."

Now all three humans converged on synthetic Number Four's spot!

"What aren't you telling us, Four," Cairo asked; a hand on one of the synthetic being's forearms. The two other humans had the same question as the former mission-lead of the original scouting mission. Only, on their faces.

"Don't worry," Four said after a pause, "what I'm about to show you was *recorded* from the scouting Tech-Housenn and I did over a day ago. It's *not* being transmitted..."

All three humans stood back, so they could see the projected recording the synthetic being had done on their mission. Hovering between all four humanoids, the live-recording showed bits of the time Number Four and Tyra were sneaking around on the outer edges of the old Ship's debris field...Number for advanced the recording so that it showed the hiding spot where Four had chosen before he threw a piece of debris a mile toward the major clumping of the debris field...

...Four paused the recording that showed a myriad of severely-clawed footprints all over the ground!

All four humans gasped upon seeing the footprints!

Charmain placed a hand on one of Cairo's shoulders. "Looks like Alexan was on to something the other day!" Referring to the last Clan Council meeting when synth Number Four had showed up that night. For it was Cairo and Luciana's youngest child that made a point about not finding footprints.

"Indeed," Number Four agreed. He, then, brought up a second projection from his contained actuator files. It was of several moving images of the Tardigrades' various species from several generations gone by. He enlarged one of the images that focused on the feet of the organism.

"Note how the clawed feet perfectly match the prints I recorded over a day ago from the old Ship's debris field." Indeed, the claws on the moving projection showed what could pass as long, curving daggers!

"Gods!" Cairo was repulsed by the eight-legged creature, with its segmented, elongated puffy body and a head the seemingly lacked a face—but for a tubular structure that most likely was its mouth!

"Charmain…Cairo," Tyra said as she took a step closer to Number Four's projections. "The *scale* of these footprints…" She cast a look at synthetic laborer Number Four's face.

"Yes," he responded, "I was hoping you'd all noticed that. Colonists, according to this recording I did of the Tardigrades' footprints, this *current* generation of this species is multiple-times *larger* than that of their ancestors!"

"If I'm using the right scale," Charmain said; leaning in to look at Four's projections better, "each one would be about the size of a new-born feline!"

"Now imagine *thousands* of *those* crawling all over your Clans' caves," the synthetic being said, with almost as much disdain as a human being!

All three humans were, now, shivering in disgust!

"Stars, *this* is why it's been so quiet between us *and* the cMaj synthetics, isn't it," Tyra asked. She kept her eyes on both projections. "I never thought I'd hear myself say this since the Synthetics' Rebellion, but all those poor synths are battling *hordes* of these—aliens!"

"Oh, but they *aren't* aliens, Madam," synth Number Four rebutted. "At least, not relative to you, humans… Remember, they were stowaways from *your* ancestors' ships an eon ago!"

"Besides," Cairo said absent-mindedly, as he watched the projections, "we're *all* the aliens on cMaj and its moons…My question is, How long do we have until these things are a threat to our Clans?"

Silence for a few seconds.

"Well, it's not like they have hover-crafts that can reach us," Tyra noted.

"We're about, what, one day's surface skimming from the crash site," Charmain asked as he looked at everyone.

"It looks like the Clan Council voted the right way in finding a settlement much farther abroad," Cairo noted somberly as he looked at Tyra. For she was the clan member that had presented the idea before the Council.

Again, there was a long patch of silence as the three humans and the synthetic being all quietly watched the ancient recordings of their new-found enemy!

"So, what do we do *now*," Tyra asked; looking around at the small band and then back at the cave; mindful that the rest of the Three Clans were asleep.

"Continue with what we voted on," Charmain said without delay. "You were right, my love…all *this* convinces me that, if anything, we need to gather our camps and head out first thing in the morning!"

Charmain noted that there was an uncomfortable silence within the small group. "Well, you all agree... right?"

Cairo shifted a bit before responding. "But let's say that the cMaj synthetics are over-taken by the Tardigrades...*all those species will, then, be the new dominate life-force on the entire planet*! Our three clan families may be technologically advanced, especially compared to *this* organism, but the numbers are on *their* side!"

"*Singularity*," Tyra simply said; her eyes locked on the projections from Number Four.

"Yes," Four said in a somber tone. "How ironic, is it not?"

Another time of quiet thinking...

Cairo said softly, in almost a singing-tone, "*But of all our achievements and of all our mastery, we've been conquered by the tiny...*"

CHAPTER SEVENTEEN

It had only been a few months ago that Councilor-Tyra Housenn Sohill had welcomed her second *great-*grandchild. And, now, she had just seen her third one upon the visit of her youngest adult child, Charl and his wife, Luciasia—daughter of Cairo an Preun and Luciana Salomenes. It was one of *their* children's new-born whom the Councilor had over at her modest stone and mortared home out in the distant plateaus from those ruins that once was a grand human colony some *fifty* years prior…

It was in those days of the sliver of the homo sapiens species on the planet of cMaj that the human population had finally started to really grow! Though there were only just over fifty humans in the re-established Settlements since the Move—thirty years ago. With each passing generation that number was compounded. It would only be a few more years before the humans finally reached the milestone of triple-digits.

Charmain, her common husband a few years after the bombing of that immense Colony during the Synthetics' Rebellion, had died a few years ago. Mostly due to a large amount of physical stress on his heart and body, from what the Colonists could tell. The Tribe had also lost the oldest of all the humans on cMaj, Cairo an Preun. It was more expected, given his advanced age at the time, especially considering all the cross-plains traveling the Tribe had gone through throughout the years. During the years after the Rebellion and at the beginning of the Move of re-settling the Clans, the Colonists' personal-flying machines were still functioning. There were six—one for each of the six original Colonists. But as the Clans' population grew, then came the re-settlement, Cairo and Charmain had let others within those clans fly the skimmers while they walked…a very considerate gesture, but one, the Colonists' suspect, contributed to both men's eventual expiration…

Half of the six artificial friends of the humans, the computerables—the portables—had all but reached their technological limits a few years ago as well. Councilor Housenn Sohill's portable was still going and two others. And the *only* synthetic being among the whole Tribe, synth laborer Number Four, was, also, still functioning. With that said, the three small, portable mechanicles and the synth were showing their many decades-old age with their scuffed-up surface, cracked transparent housings, rust, and lots of lights that no longer flickered on.

Tyra had gifted her portable to her eldest child when she was around the Age of Participation. That is to say, when a child reached the age of ten, she or he could join in the Tribe's (Clan Council many years prior) votes and meetings. Miriana, the eldest of Tyra's adult children, would have gifted *her* mother's portable to her eldest child, but by that time, even the great-computerated portable had simply suffered too much decay for such a young person to run around with. So, the Housenn Sohill clan decided to let the computerable live out its last days with its original owner. Solarvoltaic technology was highly advanced, energy-tech; especially when one took great care of the photon-based receptive portals. It was more of the *mechanics* of the portables and for synthetic laborer Number Four where they started to suffer decay.

Another reason for the homo sapiens' growth and stability in those days was due to the new, regional location they had migrated to. The distant plateaus—relative to the old Colony's ruins—had much more fertile ground. Darker, with more nutrients for the Colony's produce's seeds and general vegetation, when planet cMaj's short rainy seasons hit. Small trees began to sprout for the first time in the tiny Colony's existence! They were too young at the time to see if they would bare any fruit, but it was a true indicator that the Tribe had found much better land for them to settle on.

It helped that they had a geologist amongst their Tribe in Fillip Natsome; there to point out which terrestrial patches were best for agriculture and other geological features that showed more promise for building modest stone-housing for the growing Tribe with cMaj's moderate rains, its soils, and the many stone-features throughout the landscape...

One of the unexpected issues that the six original Colonists (then four after Cairo an Preun's and Charmain Sohill's deaths) of the Tribe had not thought of in the early days of their families on planet cMaj was the lack of other animal species! Of course, there were the Tardigrades back at the old Ship's ruins—technically, they were considered a type of *proto*-animal. From what the Tribe could speculate, the Tardigrades were able to feed off the residue of the crash site of the old Ship. The Colonists never ventured anywhere close to the debris field, especially ever since the Move.

Since the rogue synths that were left on cMaj were pretty much forced to re-locate—much like the humans!—due to the exploding population of the irradiated *and* enlarged Tardigrade species that survived the old Ship's bombing, the Colonists weren't sure what they were up to in those days, much less the surviving rogue synthetic beings on cMaj's three moons. For, unlike their human counterparts on the three moons, they did not have to worry about food nor water. However, there still was the exposure to the vacuum of space and its extreme swings from absolute freezing to boiling hot—depending on when the moons' night and day cycles. As formidable the computerated beings were, *all* synthetic beings were not omnipotent!

What they *were* able to learn about the rogue synths was from their useful friend, synthetic laborer Number Four, as he took several reconnaissance missions by himself out to the old Ship's ruins and zipped his trips in live-time...no longer restricted by the worries of the rogue synths detecting their signals as they once had. That, or, perhaps, after dealing with the unexpected onslaught of the Tardigrades it was possible the rogue synthetic laborers on cMaj simply did not want to fight a war on two fronts...

Aside from the various species of the Tardigrades hundreds of miles from the re-established settlement, all *other* animals that were on various farms and allocated land-plots from the old Colony were killed during the Synthetics' Rebellion bombing! After millions of years of evolution of each, respective, animal species' ancestral development on planet Earth many eons before, *thousands* of animal and other sentient species were *wiped out* during the Rebellion in mere seconds. *Literally*, nowhere else in the universe did those species live. So, it was a mass-extinction of many species; never to be seen again, except in the archives of the Tribe's devices and their portables and synth Number Four.

Hence, the original Colonists and their portables had to educate the children of the Three Clans of what they had just missed from the deep antiquities of their mother-planet! Many of the younger children wanted to travel to the ruins to see if they could actually find any of those Earth-based animals yet alive; roaming around the old debris-site without the humans knowing it! Needless to say, the adults and the portables had to explain to the toddlers such situation was impossible...

The elderly woman, Tyra Housenn Sohill, was the Councilor of the *officially* established township that was named after the now-defunct Colony: Vestige 2.

Years prior, while an Preun and Sohill were still alive, the Tribe had voted to continue with the human tradition of incorporating a township and all the other cultural and political aspects associated with it. Again, the Tribe had purposely stuck to that old model from the space-Colony of the nodule-government. It was the elders of the Tribes—Cairo an Preun, Fillip Natsome, Luciana Salomenes, Lanay Thuall, Charmain Sohill, and Tyra

Housenn, that all had the institutional memory of the old ways from the old Ship. And the elders, along with the portables and synth Number Four, taught the new generations how to run a government; established a, albeit, simple monetary system for the tiny Colony; schemed demarcations of land-use that was generally *within* the perimeters of the settlement; set up a court-system for any disputes that happened within the Settlement—and they were more of them, just as the population of humans grew.

All this; the very, slowly re-emerging of homo sapiens, was all under the governance of the Tribe Councilor Tyra Housenn Sohill…

"You seem bothered by something, Councilor," the old, scuffed-up portable computerated device said to Tyra. It was securely propped up against some of Tyra's personal knickknacks and miscellaneous stone tools on one of her relatively crude dressers of her domicile mastaba. They were in the commons area of the Councilor's abode; Tyra picking up a few things from the social during her son's visit with *his* grandchild and the rest of the extended family of the Housenn Sohill clan.

"Well…looking at the little ones that were just here made me think about how we should probably start on that new irrigation system," she finally said after taking a seat on one of her equally-crude chairs—though, the Colonists had taken to utilizing some of the extra vegetative husks as cushions for chairs. "Doesn't take much to use up the water we *do* have for hygiene…three more babies for the Tribe to think about now!"

"Indeed…Plus, Councilor, we still have that issue of

trying to replicate the old Ship's solarvoltaic technology. It's proven to be harder for the Colonists to pursue than we've anticipated."

The elderly woman with the long, bounded-up hair was already nodding to the portable's point. "As we all figured it would be…we just need to find a way to push our remaining jets from those personal-flyers to go a little hotter! Then we'll be able to make glass and use *that* as photonic conductors."

There was a pause from the old portable. "Councilor Housenn Sohill…what if we found some *other* way of conducting cMaj's local starlight into energy? Chemist-Salomenes and *her* family have been experimenting with the possibility of *direct* use of the sand from that tiny lake that the Thuall Clan had discovered."

She thought on the portable's question. Her lean, lined face pinching with thought. "Well, obviously anytime one converts a sun's energy directly to use *without* having to manufacture the receptors would be…" She shook her head after thinking more on it, then smiled. "Well, I've never heard such technological prospects since we were on the old Ship half a century ago! I know you, my friend…so, why are you asking me about this sand?"

"It would be nothing less than a significant jump of technological feat for this Colony since the Rebellion, as you've stated, Councilor…but there seems to be a limit to this, even *if* the an Preun Salomenes Clan were to succeed in direct-solarvoltaic conductivity. At least, in *human* principles…Councilor; the lake is occupied."

There was a space of confused quietness in the Housenn Sohill household.

"What do you mean by, *Occupied*, portable? Tardigrades?"

"No...*the sand*, Councilor Housenn Sohill..."

A soured look from the tribal chief. "What!"

Anticipating Tyra's reaction, the portable device projected recordings of moving pictions of a landscape on cMaj with a moderate-sized lake that had a meager coastline. In the projection were the four adult children of Cairo an Preun and his widow, Chemist-Luciana Salomenes; whom was a few years older than the Councilor. Some of the grandchildren helped in some of the experiments as well. The portable projected several scenes and stages of the Clan's scientific pursuits of the sands of cMaj, under the guidance of Chemist-Salomenes, utilizing yet-functioning tools from a couple of defunct single-flyers and other antique tools and equipment from the old Ship, Vestige.

"The an Preun Salomenes Clan asked me and all the other remaining computerables to document the clan's experiments with the lake's sand for the Tribe's posterity. That is, if this little colony is fortunate enough to *have* a posterity...they asked this after the Thuall Clan's discovery of how the coastline's sand that rims it would seem to shift in a matter of a few hours! The best we can tell at this point, it's almost as if the individual sand-pebbles *themselves* are moving in a flock-formation—much like bird species from our late-Colony! Only much slower, of course.

"The Thuall Clan coordinated with the Salomenes, and they were *finally* able to confirm that the sand on cMaj—at least, with *this* small lake—*is alive and sentient*!

I'm sorry to tell you a few days later, Councilor Housenn Sohill, but the an Preun Salomenes clan insisted to limit the number of people who knew about cMaj's sand—"

"Stars, the entire *tribe* would all flock there at once and who knows what the sands' reaction could be," Tyra finished out with an understanding nod.

"Precisely, Councilor..."

By that time, Councilor Housenn Sohill's mind was reeling! On top of everything else the Three Clans had survived during those decades *after* the destruction of the Colony of the *last* of the homo sapiens, now that the barest of numbers of that species was finally starting to regain some footing in civilization and technological pursuits to help boost their numbers, the Tribe *now* had a major moral issue to deal with.

In the ancients of times of human space travels, the thought of alien, sentient beings on other planets were distant fantasies for homo sapiens. But Tyra Housenn Sohill's small colony *was* the alien on cMaj and there was no fantasy-element to *any* of their situation!

"I know it's quite a bit too late to ask this," Tyra finally said after a long thought, "but why *hadn't* our computerated scans on the old Ship and our scout ships picked up their life signs when we first arrived in the cMaj system?"

"I surmise, Councilor, that as advanced as our late-colony was, they simply were too used to carbon-based lifeforms. Most likely they did not imagine the possibility of other lifeforms even being able to exist in other elemental forms..."

A silent nod from the elderly woman as she watched

the moving pictions of Luciana's family working as a professional lab team within the clan's mastaba-huts. Some of the footage were outdoors. It was the most scientific settings she had seen since the late-Colony.

"We have a lot to talk about as a Settlement, don't we, portable?" Tyra's eyes never left the projections.

"That we do, Councilor Housenn Sohill. I have to admit, I thought you would've been elated to finally *verify* that humans aren't the only, living sentient beings in the universe! If I may say so, Councilor, I don't think you realize how *proud* your ancestors would be of this little Tribe for having finally discovered life on another planet after all those eons!"

She continued to silently watch the projections hovering in the middle of her mastaba's common-space. "So, portable, my question is: If the sands on cMaj is alive, what *else* is alive on this planet we haven't even thought of? I'm no scientist, but common sense seems to dictate there are *far* more other species that are alive and sentient on a planet than just one species."

"Councilor Housenn Sohill, I had wondered that very same thing the second I received the confirmation from the an Preun Salomenes clan…"

CHAPTER EIGHTEEN

Before she scheduled a tribal meeting on the issue, the Councilor of the human colony of Vestige 2 wanted to go to the newly discovered lake found by the Thuall Clan and see for herself the sentient-sand, as they took to calling it. Over the years, Tyra and the other colonists refrained from taking their respective portable devices with them everywhere as they used to. For one, their stored data and intelligence were simply too valuable to risk losing to a clumsy move by a colonist! Also, they may have been super-advanced devices, but they, too, started to show signs of aging. It was not as if the Colonists had a repair shop around on planet cMaj to go to for parts! So, the councilor decided to leave her portable at her hut.

Many years ago, after synthetic laborer Number Four had joined the Tribe, the tribal members asked the synth if he were willing to help the humans by using its built-in jets to transport the humans around in hand-made carts that they had built for themselves as the colony started to have more young children. Number Four agreed without any hesitation.

What helped the synthetic being to agree so quickly in those days was the fact that the colonists had the ethics to approach him just as if he were a *biological* being. Obvious and logical to some, but it was *that* very issue of *how* humans had treated their synthetic labor force during the times of the great Vestige colony within the generational Ship that was at the heart of the Synthetics' Rebellion. Had there been more humans on that Ship with the same ethos of Vestige 2, cMaj would've been colonized by nearly three *million* people instead of the fifty-plus humans that were inhabiting it then.

All moot...

Just to make sure there weren't any of the colonists' old enemy of the *rogue* synthetic beings nearby—for, like Four, they were all still in fair working condition—Number Four scanned the lake's region for any kind of tech or movements. Years ago, Number Four used to hear the electronic, encrypted chatter among his fellow synthetic beings from planet cMaj to the others on those three moons. Synthetic Number Four wasn't sure if it was good news—in that the other synthetics had died out on the moons due to the naked exposure to space since there was no atmosphere on any of the moons. Or, of course, it could've also meant that the synths on the moons were keeping comm-silent...There was no practical way for any of the Colonists nor Number Four to know at that point.

Also, there, *still*, were the Tardigrades to worry about! Though the relatively new settlement was hundreds of miles from the old Ship's ruins, there was the possibility the proto-animals' various species could have migrated to the small lake's vicinity after fifty years since the Ship's bombing...not likely, but the village of Vestige 2's Tribe had to think of all scenarios if they wanted the last of the homo sapiens to survive!

Synthetic Number Four finally slowed his aging built-in rockets and set the two, back-wheels of the handcart down on the ground so he could fully roll the cart with Councilor Housenn Sohill in it. It was one of the newest pushcarts that the Colonists had built in the past few years, so it was sturdy and had more room. Indeed, the former maintenance technician from the old Colony brought along some of the last of her working equipment and tools she still had from those old days of the Ship. She didn't think she'd need them to observe the sentient-sand for herself, but she always preferred to be prepared.

The councilor and the synthetic laborer agreed that they should park the handcart *away* from the shoreline of the lake. From what Number Four had told Councilor Housenn Sohill, it was not as if the living sand were a prowling animal one had to watch out for. But neither wanted to chance it.

The two slowly walked up to the small shoreline of the small lake...it may have been a tiny body of water, especially compared to lakes of other planets and moons that were on file from the old Colony, but the two humanoid figures were still dwarfed by the scale of the lake's rimming shore that spanned miles out from them... it was a sight Tyra had not seen since the artificial lakes within the spinning Colony in the old Ship!

"You humans would have to treat the water the best you can before *bathing* with it, much less drinking it," synthetic laborer Four volunteered to the elderly woman.

For he had noticed his old human friend getting caught up in the moment of seeing such a sight! Synthetic being Number Four knew humans well enough to know what she was likely thinking after fifty years of *not* seeing a large body of water in person. "At least, until your bodies can adjust to cMaj's larger sources of water, given its elements would carry different microbes and chemicals…"

"You know, Four," the councilor finally said after a long moment studying the lake and its environs, "all those years ago when we first landed on cMaj, we were in such a hurry we didn't take the time to search out the lakes here…I know what you'll say: We had a mission of scouting out where to settle two-and-a-half million people!" She somberly shook her head. "We should've set up camp *here*, first! You realize how much time we could've saved, even as the village of Vestige 2? Instead of relying so much on cMaj's rains and extracting moister from its air with the few pieces of equipment we still have…"

Again, a regretful shaking of the head of an old woman that, now, saw so many possibilities before her, via the lake…sentient-sands be damned!

"I *do* understand your sentiments, Councilor…I scanned the lake and its immediate surroundings this time around since we're here…"

"And…?" She kept her eyes on the ecosystem in front of her.

"It's odd, Councilor, how the living sand *still* does not register as a live-signal on my scanning!"

Now her head snapped to the synthetic being. "So,

it wasn't just our ships years ago that had trouble reading them?"

"Indeed, Councilor...I'm wondering if it's due to the nature of them *being* sand?"

They were about ten yards from the shoreline. Tyra frowned at the synth's last statement. "Four...what if they *aren't* sand?"

"My scanning indicates it's a type of silica. Not quite the same as in the old Colony that originated from Earth, but it's cMaj's version of it."

"You've visited here since the Thuall clan discovered the lake, right, Number Four?"

There was the slightest of a pause from the computerable. "Yes, and if I'm anticipating where you're going, Councilor Housenn Sohill, I have not actually been *in* the sand nor touched it. I pictioned the area for records and, of course, took chemical readings of the area...but, Councilor, you've seen Chemist-Salomenes and her family experiment with samples of the sand on my recordings. The Salomenes clan would've discovered something acutely alien to us during their experiments."

Now Tyra's lined face was locked in concentration while in thought. Synthetic laborer Number Four obliged her; waiting patiently.

"Why aren't the rogue synthetics here, Number Four? Surely, with their scanning and skimming about cMaj's surface, I would think they would've discovered this lake long before us!"

Again, in an almost human-like fashion, the synthetic humanoid was slow to respond as he thought on her question. "Indeed, you are wise, Councilor Housenn

Sohill...I've operated under the *likely* assumption the other synths on cMaj *have* discovered this lake and most likely would've known about the sand's sentient qualities. We, synthetics beings—like humans—*also* utilize water as well. But for cleaning and other, more maintenance, purposes. It's probably why we don't see any signs of the rogue synthetics here. They most likely utilize it when they need it and move on. Being that we are, yet, enemies of the rogue synthetics, I don't expect them to inform us on *any* discoveries they may find."

More long thoughts from the elderly woman. "No cMaj's version of fish or other aquatic species *in* the lake?"

"Unless there are some microscopic species that aren't registering, similar to how the sand is not registering as life...otherwise, I've detected none." He directed his angular, pitted and aged head toward the calm lake. "I suppose we should venture into the shore and the water to find out for primary investigative purposes?"

"Number Four, isn't it usual in ecosystems to have more—*far more*—than *one* species in them? Predators, preys, and all that...?"

The synthetic being visibly lifted its human-like head and surveyed the lake. "Yes, Councilor. You are correct on that observation..."

"So why is there only, apparently, *one* species of a living organism in *this* particular ecosystem that's *not* showing up in your scanners, my friend?"

A small pause from Number Four. "Because, Councilor, like the rogue synthetics and myself, the sentient-sand, here, is synthetic!" He said this with almost as much emotion as a human would respond with surprise!

The old woman, Tyra, silently nodded her head; her eyes never leaving the lake before them...by that time, she *had* noticed the subtle changes of the shoreline since they had arrived there!

"So much for making our direct-solarvoltaic glassware with the sands of cMaj!"

The synthetic's head swiveled toward the councilor. "The morality of utilizing a living being—even as a *synthetic* one—for technological pursuits is but *one* of the major issues facing you and your tribe, Councilor Housenn Sohill...if we are correct about this sand being a synthetic organism, the logical follow-up is: *Who* made it and placed the organism *here*!"

Now Tyra began to shake her head and paced a few feet farther away from the shoreline. The tiny Colony was now in a conundrum that was more fitting for an advanced civilization that they were no longer apart of!

"Four, is it possible that a lifeform could *evolve* on another planet with different rules from our Mother Earth's so that such species *could* be synthetic?"

"Possible, but not likely...*we* are the aliens here, of course. But in regards to your question, if that were the case, why would only *one* species evolve as synthetic while the few vegetative species that *are* here are purely organic?"

She hadn't thought of that! Tyra nodded as she thought further on the issue.

"Probability that another, more advanced lifeform designed, constructed, and placed the sentient-sand here, Number Four?"

"Ninety-eight, point-nine percent, Councilor

Housenn Sohill," came the synth's response *without* delay that time!

She looked at him with wide eyes and stopped dead in her pacing. They both silently looked at each other, then back at the very slow-moving shoreline. For they knew what the implications of understanding the synthetic nature of the sands of cMaj meant!

CHAPTER NINETEEN

The governing councilor of the township of Vestige 2 on planet cMaj decided to *delay* a village meeting on the lake. It was one of the few times Tyra Housenn Sohill had done so since the human remnant colony had gotten together in a conference and elected Tyra as the official Councilor of Vestige 2 decades ago, just after the Tribe had re-located their Settlement hundreds of miles from the crash-site of the old Ship.

When Tyra was young, she used to make snap decisions or aggressively attacked situations. Even *after* the bombing of the Ship by the renegade synthetics of the Rebellion. But, like her eldest adult child, Mirana, had often scolded her own mother about: Tyra Housenn Sohill sometimes *still* acted as if there were a grand colony floating above cMaj—there to help the remnants of *that* Colony should things go wrong.

Even then, in her early seventies, she had to remind herself that her adult children's generation and *their* children and there after, were all born *on* cMaj and had *never* experienced living in the original Colony, Vestige. At the very least, all three of her adult children—Miriana, Janneca, and Charl—had all gotten a chance to visit the debris field of the old Ship; where the house-sized pieces of the generational ship had crashed landed.

Since the Move of the Tribe just over twenty years after the bombing, was when the original Colonists' children began to pair up and started to have *their* own children...all the offspring of the original Colonists had a completely different psychology from Tyra and her generation! They had *never* known what it was like to live in a civilization with high technology being a very part of *their* being; where, though artificially *induced*, the land's soil still had that ancient Earthy smell and the wide variety of vegetation were more numerous than the entire human population on cMaj; where the governing nodule government was just as much of a machine as the Ship itself and had tended to every needs of the Colony's two-and-a-half million citizens...All those experiences were totally alien to Tyra's generation's offspring. *They* were truly the aliens to Tyra's generation's form of existence *and* the eon of generations of humans from the old Ship...

Hence, *Councilor* Housenn Sohill had actually taken a lesson from the next generations: Be mindful that the planet that they were on, cMaj, was *it*! There was *no* giant spaceship circling the planet above that would send military help to Vestige 2, should the rogue synthetic beings decide to attack them. There was *no* colony in the millions that had spare food to ship down to them during the dry seasons on cMaj. There was *no* hospital above the atmosphere that could supply medicine or physical care for the villagers should a serious disease breakout among them...

In a word—and with total irony—the vestige of the human species on cMaj was a lot like it was when the huge

Colony was spinning within the old Ship: Out on their own out in space with no plan B…

Before Councilor Tyra Housenn Sohill and synthetic laborer Number Four returned to the Settlement, they wanted to check the lake's general vicinity for any other possible bodies of water or any other geographical features that might benefit the Colony. It took them the rest of the day, and by the time Number Four had flown Tyra back to the colonial plateau area via the hand cart, it was late evening.

Number Four had pictographically recorded their excursion for scientific and historical purposes. That, of course, included the shoreline of the lake, with its slow-moving lake-shore due to the apparent-living sand. With the aid of Tyra's portable device, which had spent the whole day recharging in cMaj's local star's light, Tyra and Number Four watched the recorded events at the lake the rest of the night as all three made scientific and everyday observations about the lake and its surrounding ecosystem.

When the trio had finished what amounted to an impromptu meeting, the councilor asked both computerables to file that recorded session that evening for her own safekeeping. Her portable asked if she wanted to share the recording of the session *and* that of Number Four's from the day, surprisingly to both computerables the councilor said no! What was more, she did not even bother to explain *why* she wanted to keep that day private.

But before cMaj's night segued into dawn, Councilor Housenn Sohill had an important mission for the synthetic being, on behalf of the entire human population…

CHAPTER TWENTY

"They went where?!" Councilor Tyra Housenn Sohill, at that point, was being *grandma* Tyra. It had been nearly two weeks since she and synthetic laborer Number Four had gone to, what was by then officially called, Lake Thuall. Now, what she had feared had *already* happened.

All three of her middle-age children were at her mastaba-hut; none of *their* children nor their grandchildren were at the councilor's home. On that day, it was *not* a social gathering! Even Tyra's portable stayed out of the family argument!

Janneca and Charl were both seated at a couple of Tyra's cMaj-wicker chair; made from one of the planet's few arboreal species. The population of said-tree exploded after the Vestige colonists migrated to the Plateau region. The two younger siblings of Mirana Housenn Thuall usually let their older sister take the lead in battling their mother when contention had arisen within the family.

"In case you haven't noticed, mom, this is a very small town, so news tends to run the circuit on cMaj," Miriana sardonically put to her mother, whom was standing across the communal area. Her hands were held out as if begging to understand. Her daughter continued. "What did you think was going to happen when you tried keeping Lake Thuall's sand a secret from the rest of us in the settlement? Just because the Thualls' progenitor is a geologist and lets *his* children and grandkids play along when he conducts experiments does not mean they're the *only* ones that should have access to the lake!"

"I knew it," Tyra shot back. "You could never get over that the majority of the villagers voted to name it after Fillip and Lanay's family! Well, young lady, even on cMaj there are unwritten rules...they found it; it gets named after—"

"—and whose idea was it to re-settle the Three Tribes all those years ago; here, on the plateaus? It was *you*, mom! If we hadn't moved in the *first* place, the Natsome Thuall clan wouldn't have stumbled across the lake!"

Tyra's eyes focused on Miriana, whom was virtually an identical twin of her mother! Just younger, and with much shorter hair. "You almost seem to forget you're talking about *your* common-law husband's father, Miri!"

Miriana glanced at her sister and brother as she rolled her eyes, but Tyra kept going. "I honestly am not sure I understand what it is you want, Miri...you think the lake should be named after us—as a family? I appreciate what you're saying about me in all this, Miri. I really do. Why, I even remember from all those years ago that you didn't even *want* to relocate the Tribes! You *voted* that we should've competed for the old Ship's ruins against the rogue synths!" Tyra said this as she shot her eyes toward Janneca and Charl; as if to remind them and get them to not back Miriana on the issue.

Miriana went silent but shook her head as she sighed.

"Totally a different issue, mom, and you *know* it…Look, all this is too late anyway. The majority of the town's adolescent citizens have learned about it and have been taking portion-cups of the sand and making them into pets, mom…" Here, Miriana actually smirked. "Maybe we were a little *too* efficient in how we taught them about the old Colony's animal populations!"

Despite themselves, everyone in the councilor's abode began to laugh at Miriana's observation!

"You realize this will make using the sand for direct-solarvoltaic materials impossible, now," Charl said after the laughter died in the hut. Like everyone else in Vestige 2 during the current windy season, he was swaddled in thin clothing made from cMaj's sturdy vegetative materials that blocked much of the planet's course dust in the air.

"Why should that matter," Miriana rebutted. "It's a technology the Settlement needs…we can't have something like a novelty such as *moving sand* get in the way of that."

Everyone else in the mastaba's communal room glanced at one another.

"You can't be serious, Miri," Janneca finally voiced from her seat; swathed in her drab, thin body-wrap clothing. "*They're sentient, Miriana*…synthetic or not!"

"What's next," Charl input, "our computerables?"

Tyra shook her head in disappointment as she subconsciously glanced at her old friend the portable! Whom deliberately remained silent during the whole exchange.

"Don't take me out of context," Miriana replied;

pointing an accusatory finger at her siblings. "Even during mom and dad's time in the old Ship when they were young, there used to be *hundreds of thousands* of Colonists that ate animal flesh—and *those* species were closer to humans than some synthetic sub-species in an elemental form!"

The councilor, Janneca, and Charl all reluctantly gave intimated looks...indeed, Tyra had to admit to herself, Miriana *was* right about that!

"So," Charl said with a heavy sigh after a long silence within the hut, "what do we do now?"

"We continue as we always do," Councilor Housenn Sohill shot back with no hint of doubt. "I'll schedule a tribal meeting so we can all get the same information from the Natsome Thuall clan's research into the sand... plus, I'll have something very important to present to you all..."

All three of the Housenn Sohill adult children looked toward their mother and tribal leader. She nodded in response.

"It'll be the biggest proposition I'll have done for us all since the Move!"

The three offspring gave uneasy glances.

"And, yes, it has a lot to do with Lake Thuall's discovery. But for now, I'll make us all some dinner..."

CHAPTER TWENTY-ONE

The scream was so sharp it caused the elderly woman to fall out of her wicker bed and onto her mastaba-hut's floor. It was a good thing Tyra kept a high-quality, thick rug that one of her grandchildren had crafted and gifted her under her cot; for it softened her landing!

"I detect no rogue synthetics, Councilor Housenn Sohill," her old portable volunteered for her, for he knew that would be her first question.

"Thanks, portable!"

After quickly wrapping her comfortably clothed body with a more public wrap, Tyra ran out of her hut and straight toward the scream in cMaj's windy night! The township of Vestige 2 had developed a network of connecting walkways that were mostly a clear path via natural pedestrian traffic. She utilized the walkway system—lit up by a few solarvoltaic light-pieces. By the time the councilor passed the center of the spreading mastaba-huts and domicile patchworks of projects spread throughout the Colony, there was a second scream!

By that time, the majority of the township was out on the crossways; some of the Colonists brandishing hand-made weapons!

"It's alright, sisters and brothers," Geologist-Fillip Natsome—the eldest of the entire Tribe—countered the three scores or so of villagers as they sought out an enemy; frantically looking around the Settlement with their sophisticated spears, axes, and crossbows! There were a few times over the fifty years since the original Colonists had to fight off the rogue synthetic beings on cMaj after the Synthetics' Rebellion up to more recent years, so the villagers of Vestige 2 had a long history of combat and weapon-manufacturing!

Standing next to the slender, old geologist was one of his and Lanay Thuall's adult sons, Lannel and his common-law wife. It was Lannel's children—Natsome's grandchildren—that were the ones that had done the screaming! Lanay's daughters and sons were gathered around him and his common-wife; all looking toward their mastaba-hut as they squeezed against the middle-agers.

"It's not the synthetics—" Fillip started; yet keeping both hands held up as he tried to calm down the crowd—indeed, there was a time that the survivors of the *original* Vestige colony would've thought humanity would *never* again see such slowly growing numbers!

"Yes, we know," one of the younger male villagers from the Housenn Sohill clan shot back. "The portables informed us already…what's the problem?"

"*Tardigrades*," one of the geologist's grandchildren spoke up; her finger jutting out toward the lit hut; its front door closed with large rocks blocking it, presumably in case the door's fashioned-lock had not held up to the unnaturally, enlarged proto-animals! To Tyra, it seemed a bit overly done, given the Tardigrades' species had gotten bigger due to the radiation from the old ship's enclosed sector, but they weren't exactly bears, either!

"—Stars' gravity!"

"—those damn Synthetics…they brought them here!"

"—What good will our analogue weapons be against *thousands* of those?"

"About how many did you see," Tyra finally asked as she quickly stepped up and joined the family.

"Councilor," Fillip Natsome quickly greeted her with a snap of his head. He then cast his attention to his son. For it was *his* family's home.

"Councilor…I'd say about twenty!"

"—probably just the vanguard."

"—Better check all huts tonight!"

"—thought I heard some scratching last night!"

"—gods!"

"Well, it *has* been about thirty years since we've first seen them at the ruins," Tyra said absent-mindedly; her eyes on Lannel's family's mastaba–hut in the windy night. The three, mixing clans that made up the Tribe were mummering behind her. She glanced over her shoulder, to get the attention of the Tribe. "Honestly, sisters and brothers, I'm guessing this is just a natural migration of the Tardigrade species *from* the old Ship's ruins…I was afraid this would happen one day!"

"Councilor," came Chemist-Luciana Salomenes's voice from farther back in the crowd, "can we have synthetic laborer Number Four stand guard for us tonight?"

There was a noticeable pause from Tyra. She turned

to face the two-thirds of the whole township of Vestige 2 that were there; retrograde weapons drawn, the people in a tense posture! "I ask that we set up *your* portable, Luciana; *your* portable, Miriana; and, of course, I'll set up *mine* as well, to keep a scanning watch over the village. I have Number Four on an important task."

Tyra's family all knew this from the most recent family argument they had over at the Councilor's hut a couple of days ago! But the rest of the Colonists that were there all cast confused glances toward each other! But none protested.

'Yes, Councilor,' came the chorused responses from the chemist and Tyra's eldest adult child.

As cMaj's seasonal strong wind blew that late-evening, Councilor Housenn Sohill looked about the villagers as they began to disperse—Lannel and his wife in a conversation with Fillip, arranging how the whole family could stay at his and Lanay Thuall's hut for the night while the Tardigrades were playing guests that night! "Could everyone please wait for a bit...?"

The nearly forty colonists all stopped at once...a bit eerie, Tyra thought. Indeed, in some ways, after all those decades on cMaj and as Vestige 2's leading colonist, she *still* sometimes felt uncomfortable with her power over the remnant of the human species!

"I was planning on telling everyone this during our next tribal meeting—which I've yet to even schedule!" There were some polite laughs. The winds flung everyone's long body-wraps and hair about as Tyra thought more on her words and turned to face Miriana; standing within a knot of the colonists. "Long before any of *our* children and their children were born, there were *six* original colonists from the original Colony, and four of us were members of that old system called the nodule government—including me…

"Something like a year *before* the Ship arrived at cMaj, the nodule took a vote on if we should even bother to tell the colonists about the Ship's system automatically adjusting the planet-like conditions within the O'Neillian sector of the Ship. The majority voted *no*; I voted that we *should*…even after all those years, sisters and brothers, I've always felt it was an unjust vote for a small group of people to vote to keep almost *three million* people in the dark over the governing nodule changing the Colony's planetary conditions! The nodule's intentions were well-meaning, that I remember. But…"

Tyra shook her head. Remembering the events when she was a young woman in her twenties at that time. And, now, when she looked around at the Colonists that were around her, she had *grandchildren* about that age! "Intentions are not tangible; it's what we do, affirmed? Well…now, I had found *myself* doing the same thing, in principal…I'm sure everyone here knows about the unique qualities of Lake Thuall's sand by now?"

There were nods of consent; smiling faces watching her silently. Tyra continued as she nodded and shrugged.

"Alright…I'm just going to throw this out there *now* while the majority of the villagers are here. Based on official Vestige 2's laws, we have a clear quorum: I make note that we open Lake Thuall to *all* Colonists, *but* with a warning that they go cautiously; as we *still* don't know much about the sentient-sand…"

The Councilor paused, then looked around at the silent colonists. Clearly, some couldn't believe they were taking an actual vote, literally, in the middle of the township in the middle of the night, after they had just dealt with Tardigrades! But, indeed they were, and those present had voted unanimously for the Councilor's noted statement!

In an almost surreal setting, the Colonists present began to applaud the results of the vote! There were some small talk and quips, but Councilor Housenn Sohill had at least one more order of business for the impromptu tribal meeting...

"I sent synthetic laborer Number Four on a peace mission..."

Silence...except for the seasonal winds of cMaj.

"I'm sorry, Councilor," one of the adult grandchildren of the Natsome Thuall clan finally spoke up, "what do you mean by *peace* mission? Is that when the victims of attacks give into their assailants' demands and the victims give up some of their land...?"

Obviously, the young man was being sarcastic, but the thrust of his retort was *exactly* how most Colonists felt! Indeed, all the positive outreach that Councilor Housenn Sohill had done that late night and her having conducted an historic vote for the tiny Colony was *all* undone after her last short statement!

Some of the Colonists were actually *yelling* at the councilor! Others just looked at her as they slowly shook their heads...in some ways, Tyra thought to herself, they were *worse* than those yelling at her. One didn't know if they were planning an assassination!

The commotion after the Councilor's announcement of the peace mission to the rogue synthetic beings on cMaj had gotten so bad, the rest of the Colonists that had stayed behind in their respective mastsaba-huts had ran out to see what was going on! But she had to re-take control of the escape pod, otherwise known as the Vestige 2 settlement!

"Listen! You all know the sentient aspects of the sand on the lakeshore at Lake Thuall! I had a long meeting with Number Four and my portable about the lake and its sand after Four took me around and recorded the whole trip…after examining the pictions and other data on the sand, *there is no way such sentient being could evolve on its own on a planet*! Sisters and brothers, are you understanding what I'm saying?

"The data that synth Four and I collected several days ago show that either there is another intelligent species *right now* on cMaj and we don't know who, what, and where they are, *or* historically speaking there used to be such an intelligent civilization on this planet and they left or died out—leaving the living sand here on cMaj by itself!"

Well that got the Tribe's attention!

"Are you understanding now, sisters and brothers…? We were still in the process of studying the lake and its sand, so I can't tell you for sure if it's *only* Lake Thuall with the living sand, or if it's planet-wide…But this is why I've decided to send Number Four to *try* to strike a conversation with the rogue synths: *If* it is so that whatever species had created and placed the sentient-sand on cMaj *is* still here, based on the historical research Four, my portable, and I have done, typically, the more advanced civilization—ironically—will feel threatened and enslave and/or destroy the less advanced society…"

Tyra looked around the, now, silent village. That time, the entire population was there in the night as the wind kept buffering the colonists. She went on.

"In case you haven't noticed, my sisters and brothers, we aren't exactly at gods-status since the Synth Rebellion! Look, we *can't* do this on our own *if* there is an advanced civilization on this planet—not with our population *now*…" Tyra shrugged. "The way I figured, all of the synthetic beings that are on cMaj have something like another thirty years left in *their* life-cycle. *If* we and they continue to maintain good computerable hygiene practices. Of course, some of *us* will have passed away by then, but our little colony would have a *much* better fighting chance than if we continue to inch forward as a species instead of taking long, striding steps!"

There were very long, silent glances exchanged within the Colony after that. They all did not need to say it—again! But truth was, the vestige of humanity *owed* Councilor Tyra Housenn Sohill a *lot*! Over fifty years prior, it was her search crew under her command that had found the alarm that alerted the governing nodule system that the old Ship was low on nuclear fuel—and from *that* mission, it lead to Vestige's ship diverting to planet cMaj.

Twenty year after the Rebellion and the homo sapiens species came within six human individuals from literal extinction and it was Tyra Housenn Sohill who came up with the plan to migrate the Three Tribes to the plateau region—a gamble, true. But it paid off greatly with a region richer in soil, more solid rock-structures for housing and making tools, and hundreds of miles between the burgeoning Colony and both the rogue synthetic beings *and* the Tardigrades!

And, now, that *same* Colony—which had grown just shy of ten times its population since the day of the old Ship's bombing—was being asked to trust that same woman on the next chapter of the human species' recovery from oblivion with trying to have a peace treaty between that Colony and those same synthetics...

CHAPTER TWENTY-TWO

" **...i**t's working!" Filleppe Natsome Thuall, one of the two middle-age sons of Geologist-Fillip Natsome and former pilot of the original Vestige colony, Lanay Thuall, was in the specially built structure that was solidly crafted from cMaj's plateau-stones. It was the township's only laboratory. It had only taken the villagers a couple of weeks to find the right stones and bush-branches to construct it.

Geologist-Natsome and Chemist-Luciana Salomenes an Preun—the last two scientists from the original survivors of the old Ship's bombing—both scurried to where the scientist-in-training had been testing out how some of the acquired sentient-sand from Lake Thuall was reacting to signals being sent from Luciana's own portable...the incredible thing was the direct-solarvoltaic properties typically found in glass or materials similar to glass was, at that time, found in the *yet*-living sentient-sand...

In other words, at least at that point in the team's experiments with the sand, there was *no need* to kill the living sand in order to achieve solar empowering energy from the sentient-sand!

"How is this even possible," Vestige 2's councilor,

Tyra Housenn Sohill, asked as she watched from a distance from the work area of the stone lab; making sure not to get in the way of the three scientists.

Luciana replied; keeping her eyes on the moving sand within the lab's somewhat crude worktable, "Well, partially due to natural tropism—which makes me wonder if there are some vegetative elements to the sand...Essentially, Councilor, the sand is able to conduct cMaj's local star photons and any *other* energy almost the same way the human body is a semiconductor. But even better! What gets me, Councilor, is *how* this synthetic species is able to take our signals and super-simultaneously express those signals—and it does not matter the distance between us *and* the sand!"

Tyra looked at her old friend with a shocked face. Geologist-Natsome and his scientific-protégé middle-age son both smiled as they began to set up a demonstration for Councilor Housenn Sohill on the wide slab of cMaj stonework.

"Luciana," Tyra said; making sure she understood while the three scientists worked at the demonstration, "are you saying that I could be five miles from that portion of sentient-sand and send signals to it, it will *instantly* receive my signals—as if there were no distance between us?"

"Councilor...I'm saying that, if *you* were on one of cMaj's moons *you* would have the absolute ability to make this thing crawl—instantly!—by sending commands; with the proper connections in terms of physics, of course..."

Tyra froze on the spot with such news! Even during the old days when Luciana, Fillip, and Tyra lived in the original

Vestige colony with all its scientific and technological miracles, the Councilor had *never* encountered this type of technology where it utilized a synthetic being and one was able to harness a star's power in order to operate as an *astronomical* puppet-master! The potential applications for such technology were astonishing!

All four went silent after they walked over and joined Councilor Housenn Sohill at her corner of the lab. None of the colonists in the stone laboratory were even close to the sentient-sand that was on the worktable. It was a way for them to conduct the experiments and practice without anyone who were to watch the recorded pictions having to say the scientists had cheated somehow.

Chemist-Salomenes glanced at Tyra. "And we *are* recording all our endeavors, Councilor. I know how important that is to you…Portable," the chemist said with her voice raised a bit, for it was propped up on the ledge of a wall within the lab, "please send a command to the sand-portion to jump about five inches to its left."

"Complying," the portable's old, scratchy actuator voice responded.

No later than five seconds the sentient-sand, at approximately one ounce, *leapt* to its side to the left—its granular properties moving like dry water! Councilor Housenn Sohill flinched and caught young-Filleppe by his arm—startled to see something, *literally*, so alien move in such a way!

"*By my star's gravity…*" Tyra didn't ask for permission— she slowly walked over to the open worktable and visually examined the portion of sand that, now, was inert. Behind her, humanity's vestige of science were smiling and even tearing up at the achievement!

"Too bad our cerebral-comms gave out years ago... Could you imagine us using the comms; almost like super-humans, able to control *swaths* of sand just by *thought*," Tyra quipped, though half-serious! The three scientists laughed at her comment. She went silent and focused on the sentient-sand again. "Portable, please instruct the sand to leap into my hand—"

"—Uh, Councilor..."

"—Tyra, that's not what we planned!"

"—Councilor!"

"Complying," Luciana's portable said, ignoring the protestations from the scientists and sent a tiny shot of photonic-data to the sand!

The small amount of cMaj sand jumped off the open worktable and straight into the Councilor's hands! Luciana, Fillip, and Filleppe all stood in silence while their councilor examined the synthetic sand in her hands...it slowly shifted within her cupped hands; not a drop of its granules being left behind.

Tyra simply and slowly replaced the sand onto the workstation and took a couple of steps back from the table; rubbing her hands together, ensuring that none of the sand stuck to her.

"Chemist-Salomenes...Geologist-Natsome...General Scientist-Natsome, this marks a key moment for this small human settlement..."

All three nodded behind Tyra, not saying a word. She continued.

"I'd like for all your recorded pictions to be catalogued

and shared with the two other portables *and* synthetic Number Four, if you could, portable?"

"Complied, Councilor," Luciana's device said after a few seconds of Tyra's request.

"There is an ancient saying," the older Natsome scientist said after a moment of quiet thinking from the group, "The blade has at least two side *and* can cut either way…I can't help but think what the Councilor and Number Four said about the likely origins of cMaj's sand after *their* own research!"

So much for the glory of discovery!

"You know," young Filleppe said, "my wife and our children had a long discussion about that a week ago… wouldn't we have seen *some* kind of indicator of a more advanced civilization by now?" He shifted his eyes to his father. "I, also, have an ancient saying for us to think on— one of my favorites from the sciences that you, father, and the portables have taught my generation: the Paradox of the Fermi! If such advanced civilization exists on cMaj, most likely we would've seen them by now!"

The chemist shifted uneasily on her feet. "Not necessarily…as long as our colony has been on cMaj, we *still* haven't been everywhere on this *continent*, let alone the rest of the planet!"

"Fifty years, and not even you *original* Colonists have seen a domestic civilization that could've created the sentient-sands," Filleppe rebutted; his eyes squinting with incredulity.

Indeed, it was a point that resonated with the elders around him. They all looked off to some corner and nodded to themselves.

"I still find it hard to believe that such a synthetic sub-species could evolve naturally," Luciana volunteered; her eyes back on the small mound of sand on the worktable. She shook her head. "It's going to take some time to figure *this* one out!"

"If ever," the younger Natsome scientist pointed out. Again, nods of consent.

"I don't know about you scientists," Councilor Housenn Sohill said after a short pause, "but I think we could utilize the sand *against* the Tardigrades!"

Geologist-Natsome was already nodding his head. "I was thinking about that, too, Councilor! Perhaps build some kind of wall around the village...fortify it with sentient-sand in such a way that we could use the sand's properties to *block* the Tardigrades from getting *into* to the Settlement!"

The others voiced agreements.

"That is the most plausible usage of the sand I've heard from anyone within the village, yet," Luciana's portable stated. "Aside from the super-simultaneous application for energy and communications, of course."

"Thanks, portable," the young scientist said with a nod of his head.

That was all Councilor Housenn Sohill needed to hear. "Then we should start right away on figuring out *how* to harvest the sand from Lake Thuall and transport it back to the township...I'll talk with some of the other colonists about it while you three continue the science end of it."

The three scientists chorused a 'Thank you, Councilor,' and went back to work on the project with the sands they had on stock within the stone laboratory.

CHAPTER TWENTY-THREE

"...**T**hey're here, Councilor Housenn Sohill," synthetic laborer Number Four told her in a whispered, electronic voice. He had just gotten back from his once-secret mission that Vestige 2's councilor had sent him on. Number Four had been staying in contact with Tyra via her portable device, but outside of that none of the Colonists had seen the synthetic being for about two weeks.

They were in Councilor Housenn Sohill's mastaba-hut. It was very late at night and she kept her solarvoltaic lamps dimmed so none of the other Colonists could see that she was up and about...over the years, they learned if they saw the Councilor's lights on late at night it usually meant that the councilor was up to something in regards to the Settlement's business!

"Good...where are they staying for now?"

"I showed them the caves just south of here..."

Tyra, swaddled in her domestic body-wrap and seated in one of her handmade wicker chairs, nodded to herself in the darkened hut. "Three of them, right?"

"Correct, Councilor...perhaps it is a small matter, but they anticipated the humans would have trouble distinguishing them from each other, so they've taken to being *named*!"

Tyra flinched out of surprise!

"Well, that *is* encouraging," her portable said from a nearby table. "What are their names, synthetic Number Four?"

"Number Two is Majoreen, Number Three is Forward On, and Number Five is Ascent...these are the names they all wish for Vestige 2 villagers to address them by. Again, with the hopes of showing good-will toward the humans."

Tyra's silence was palpable.

"If I may, Councilor Housenn Sohill," her portable said; sympathy in his raspy actuator voice, "you seem hesitant. This was, in fact, your idea...I hope you realize I am *not* criticizing when I say this."

"Oh, no, portable...I understand where you are coming from..." Now the elderly woman got up and did her famous pacing within the dark of her hut. "I just... well, both of you know how we, humans, are...we are not like either of you, two. Forgiving and working with a group of people—or synthetics—that had committed extreme violence toward them *has* been achieve by few in human history. But, in practice, my friends..." Tyra shook her head non-stop for a while.

"Literally, *millions* of humans, animals, and even hundreds of thousands of *your* fellow synths and portables had *all* been destroyed by a rebellion in which *these three* synthetics were all apart of! I'm afraid I'm hoping too much from my people to—if not forgive, at the very least move on! I...I don't know, my friends...I think this may not work!"

The portable said nothing. Nor did the synthetic laborer. Human-induced creations or not, both yet managed to come across as really *listening* to the human... which was far more than what Tyra's fellow human beings often did!

It remained silent in the Housenn Sohill mastaba-hut for a while. Tyra kept pacing, working her mouth as she partially covered it with one of her hands.

"Tyra," the portable said to her after a while—a very rare occasion that he used her first name, "perhaps we should *not* do this right now. After all, the rest of the Colony doesn't know about their presence near the township. Also, today was meant to be an introductory step. As you've alluded to earlier, Councilor, a nice gesture, but not substantive."

"I have to admit to *both* of you," synthetic laborer Number Four said; never having moved from his standing position, "I truly believe this is the only way forward— especially more for the *humans* than it would be for the rogue synthetics! We, synths, *aren't* gods, to use humans' folklore-references, but we are far better-adapted to live on cMaj than the homo sapiens species. Of course..." For dramatic effect, the synthetic being lifted one of his forearms and displayed his weathered arm—pitting and rust visibly starting to spread on the once-glossy, human-like arm! Number Four utilized a tiny bit of his internal light-source to illuminate his forearm, so the human could see. "We, too, have a time limit...

"But I *do* see your portable's point, Councilor Housenn

Sohill. It would be non-productive for *all* of us to have survived the Synthetics' Rebellion all those decades ago and end up perishing at the hands of each other in a fit of primitive savagery! We've waited this long, Councilor Housenn Sohill, we can all afford to wait a bit longer, still…"

The two synthetics saw that the human had tears upon Tyra stopping her pacing and facing them. She silently nodded her head and slowly walked over to the door to her hut to, politely, open it for Number Four. She thought about how good it was to have synthetic, actuated beings in times such as what she was facing. Humans were simply too predictable and emotionally bound to even *hope* for an objective conversation about a peace treaty; much less craft one!

"Tyra!"

It was Number Four! He had called out to her just seconds after leaving her mastaba-hut…it was even rarer for him to use the councilor's first name than her old and trusted portable!

Tyra quickly grabbed her portable—a villager on cMaj never knew when they might need one!—and ran out of her hut and into the night…

Several feet away were the three synthetic beings, Majoreen, Forward On, and Ascent. All, similar to their human counterparts, wrapped up in body-wraps to protect them against the planet's non-stop winds. And surrounding *them*, in a semi-circle, was the entire human population in all of the universe…

Tyra's eyes were wide-open with surprise! The elderly

woman looked as if she ran into an invisible wall as she stopped in her tracks!

"Oh, my," was all that her portable could say.

For a long while, in the midst of all the humans and all the synthetics, nothing but the wind was heard that night…

"Our other portables detected the synthetics as they approached the village," Miriana, Tyra's eldest adult child, informed. She was toward the front of the human-cluster; her *own* family standing next to her.

The Councilor merely nodded as she looked out at the populace. Then she looked at synthetic laborer Number Four; not sure what to think!

"So, what does this mean," Tyra asked aloud, over the wind. "Are we willing to try this? Because all I see, right now, is the vestige of our Mother Earth…"

VOLUME TWO

TWENTY YEARS LATER. . .

CHAPTER TWENTY-FOUR

"**They** did what?!" Councilor Miriana Housenn Thuall exclaimed over her refurbished comm. Long-gone were the cerebral-comm days of the *original* Vestige society of that once immense colony of well-over two million citizens. The last generation was of her late-mother's, Tyra Housenn Sohill, some 70 years ago…when the generational starship's synthetic humanoids rebelled against the humans and bombed the 20-mile-long ship with just a few scouting ships! It was the remnant nuclear fuel within the ancient sector of the generational ship that had done the Colony in. If it weren't for the relatively small amount of nuclear substance in the original section of Vestige, the descendants of the starship believe the planet, cMaj, would have had a human population closer to *three* million at that time instead of the mere-approximate 250 humans…on the entire planet!

"It is correct what you heard, Councilor Housenn Thuall," Fuegon, the young spy, said. His young face was zip-cast on the Councilor's hand-held communicator, which utilized cMaj's sand for photovoltaic glass and nearly rivaled the technology of *original* Vestige—just without the holographic projections. "The Dominionists

Clan was successful in reaching the other side of the planet, ma'am! And Janneca was able to confirm it!"

Councilor Housenn Thuall's head snapped to the side, apparently needing time to think of the implications of one of the rival Clans making such an historic feat on cMaj! Not since the starship's bombing some 70 years prior had *any* human survivor taken flight! Not that the surviving humans on cMaj did not know *how* to fly—that is, with engineered craft. Indeed, the Three-Clans society of homo sapiens were not "primitive," they were marooned. The trick was for the humans to either venture several hundreds of miles away to the crash-site of the old Ship and risk nuclear exposure from the Ship's ruins. *Or* take possibly a hundred years for the tiny population to re-gain the ability to fly; like their ancient ancestors had done, back in the Sol system, on Earth—thousands of years ago!

Councilor Thuall's grandchildren were over at her mastaba-hut for the day and were running around outside and trampolining all over her garden! It was the hut Miriana Housenn Thuall had inherited after her mother—the *first* Councilor of Vestige 2 settlement, Tyra Housenn Sohill—had died. That was about 13 years ago. Right after her mother's death, the now-dissolved Tribe of Vestige 2 had voted for her eldest child, Miriana, to take her vacant, governing position. Sadly, a few years after that, the Tribe broke up between the natural, cultural fault lines of the three original Clans from the early days after the bombing of Vestige...

So, in addition to worrying about the three, rogue surviving synthetic humanoids having recently achieved flight with remnant-parts from the old ship of Vestige, *now* the Vestige Clan had to compete against the Dominionists Clan for flight—and based on the new reporting, the Dominionists had beaten the Vestige Clan! The one certain thing that the aging clan Councilor could count on was *not* worrying about the cMaj Clan achieving flight. For *their* culture and code of ethics grounded them with the lifestyle of mostly using natural materials within that clan's natural surroundings.

"Councilor," young-Fuegon prompted Miriana over the static-prone transmission of her reconstructed comm-device. Apparently, she had gotten lost in her thoughts.

"Let's be honest, Fuegon; we've all known the synths would reach flight at some point, given their advanced abilities compared to us-humans—"

"—Well, they can't *really* be all that smart; they're slowly debilitating, Councilor. Partially because they were stupid enough to fool with all that irradiated materials at the crash-site!"

"True! But the *synths* are the ones with more influence on this planet than all of us humans, now! Look at us, Fuegon; humans can't even agree to come together to construct an edifice-of-common during holidays; did you really think any of the Clans stand a chance against the synths? Don't worry, child, the Dominionists may have reached the other side of cMaj, but it's a fool's pursuit without a viable plan for colonizing over there!"

The young man's face gave a bit of a scoffing look over the comm. "Councilor, with respect, ma'am, you sound resigned to being beaten by the synths and *now* the Dominionists!"

There was a jab of irritation within the Councilor. She walked several yards away from her frolicking grandchildren in the garden. "Fuegon, just say what's on your –"

"—It's on *most* of our Clan members' minds, Councilor Housenn Thuall…we cannot afford to take it for granted that cMaj is such a large planet that there is plenty of room for all three Clans *and* the synths! Most clan members are telling me they want a more robust plan from you, ma'am."

"What, you mean like a plan to over-run the Dominionists *and* the cMaj Clans and then we all become one, big happy Tribe like in the old days of my mother? And then we march hundreds of miles to Vestige's crash-site and start cobbling some kind of vehicle that can fly us all over the planet? While in the meantime, we would begin to get *mysterious* ailments from the radiation…

"Fuegon, did you think I was joking when I said we, humans, cannot even agree to build a facility for a common use amongst humans! There is no way in stars we'll be able to do this fantasy you and some of your friends in our Clan want us to do!"

The young man's face morphed into a steely look. "May I suggest the Councilor also not take for granted her position…there is nothing to say in our Clan's charter that the position of Councilor is necessarily inherited."

Councilor Housenn Thuall flinched, as if doused by cold water! "Young man, are you threatening me?"

"Of course not, Councilor…you have my honor as being the torch-bearer of our first Councilor. I'll report when I have more news…good day, Councilor."

Miriana did not even bother to respond. She stowed the comm-device into one of her body-wrap's pockets and went back to be with her grandchildren playing in her garden, smoke coming from the hut's chimney given it had been cool weather the past week.

CHAPTER TWENTY-FIVE

Filleppe Natsome Thuall, Councilor Miriana Housenn
Thuall's common law husband, was the son of
the geologist that was on the scouting party with the
Councilor's mother, Tyra. Geologist-Natsome died a few
years before Councilor Tyra Housenn Sohill. The *Thuall*
came from the geologist's surviving widow, Lanay Thuall,
whom was the pilot of the scouting ship that brought the
six original Vestige scouting crew. And, hence, the vestige
of humanity. Lanay Thuall, in her nineties in the days of
Councilor Miriana Housenn Thuall, was alive and well,
though she did not get around too often. She was the last
of the original Vestige colonists.

In the days of the old colony of the starship Vestige,
common law marriages or relationships of the spouses or
partners were flexible about adopting family names upon
the union of each respective relationships. Lanay's late-
husband, Geologist-Fillip Natsome, had spearheaded the
scouting of the plateaus some 20 years ago, with his own
family and they had all discovered what became known as
Lake Thuall. Known among the humans for the shoreline's
"sentient-sand," though there still were unknown factors
of whether or not the living sand naturally evolved or was

placed there by a previous, advanced civilization that was nowhere to be seen on cMaj!

For several years it was a source of contention within the former Tribe, and it was because of the mere naming of the lake after one Clan that had contributed to the breakup of the Tribe.

The other main reason for the dissolvement of the original Tribe was the *rejection* of a peace deal between the humans and the synthetic laborer humanoids that were left on cMaj after the Synthetic Rebellion on Vestige. It was a gamble by Councilor Tyra Housenn Sohill, herself, and one that she had lost. For the memory of the remaining *other* original Vestige colonists of the bombing of their planet-ship by rogue synthetics was simply, still, too strong. After all, nearly two and a half *million* humans had perished that night. Plus, not every computerable humanoid agreed with the Rebellion! So, there were likely hundreds of thousands of *them* that, also, were obliterated in the bombing via the scouting teams' four ships—stollen by the synthetics that were part of the scouting mission on cMaj and the planet's three moons. The scouting vehicles were converted into missiles via the hands of synthetics from the scouting crews and the antiquated nuclear fuel left over were the ingredients for the end of a noble mission of Vestige…at first, *unknown* to the Ship's citizens and crew that its mission was to *preserve* the homo sapiens species. Due to some solar system-wide war an eon ago in Mother Earth's local star system, as was discovered by a young Tyra Housenn and her late-portable device.

The cMaj Clan, the smallest clan in terms of

population, was formed as a result of the old Tribe's vote *against* the peace deal with the synthetics. In terms of temperament and philosophy, the small group of humans within the former Tribe were from all three cultural clans, which would eventually lead to the Vestige Clan, the Dominionists Clan, and the first-formed cMaj Clan... cMaj members were the most spiritual and religious-minded within the human population on planet cMaj. They were the least contentious of the three Clans and the least powerful, especially given their rejection of modernism, relative to the original Colony of starship Vestige.

The Vestige Clan, tied to the Housenn Thuall lineage, was the faction that held onto the old ways of the original Colony the most—from the Clan's structure of voting system to the cultural norms from the old Ship, Vestige.

The Dominionists Clan were just that: the Clan with an emphasis on the Human being as opposed to the planet-based ideals of the cMaj Clan. The two other Clans often accused the Dominionists of being *Dominionistic*—with an attitude that planet cMaj was merely a source meant for utilizing at homo sapiens' will and the rogue synthetics had no right to dominate the planet nor the humans...Which was part of the reason *why* the communique that Councilor Housenn Thuall had with the young spy, Fuegon, was so important: Now that Clan Dominionists had the power of flight—along *with* the synthetic humanoids, with the Dominionists' philosophy, there was bound to be the first warfare on planet cMaj between the two groups!

Then there was one lone tribe, all on his own. A

synthetic being, no less. Synthetic laborer Number 4. He was the *only* synthetic on cMaj that was *not* a "rogue synth"—the mere other three were a tiny population, but each one equivalent to three humans, in terms of strength and even *more* so in terms of intellectual agility.

Number 4, who warned the original human scouting colonists of the rogue synths' on-coming rebellion, was a close friend of Councilor Mariana Housenn Thuall's mother, Tyra. He was appointed by Councilor Tyra Housenn Sohill to mediate her peace deal with the rogue synthetics on cMaj! It was *never* popular with the greater majority of the original colonists. So when the former Tribe had voted against the peace deal, Synth Number 4 saw it a waste of *his* time to remain with the humans. Yet, Number 4 was not of the same philosophy as the rogue synths... So, he remained in solitude. He never told the humans where he resided, and it had only been, perhaps, two or three times that any of the humans had spotted the slowly aging synthetic humanoid. And even then, it was from a distance, while the humans were out gathering cMaj's fruits from the planet's small species of trees, or while they were exploring other parts of the continent, they would get a tiny glimpse of the tall, clothed synthetic being.

Councilor Miriana Housenn Thuall counselled within herself that she could really use synthetic laborer Number 4's help at that moment, with the two new air-powers that were on their way to some kind of war...

CHAPTER TWENTY-SIX

Beeshmah Salomenes worked directly for Councilor Miriana Housenn Thuall and kept that private within her own family, much less the rest of the Vestige Clan. Since the Councilor had family over at her mastaba-hut for a few days, Beeshmah had to meet the older woman elsewhere. Beeshmah still lived with her parents and had several siblings, so *her* abode was out of the question. Councilor Housenn Thuall had the young woman rendezvous with her at one of the very raggedy plateaus that had towering rock formations and tended to block localized signals...that was a deliberate part on the Councilor's end!

The towering outcrops was a region that many lovers used to get away from the growing human societies on cMaj and, frankly, contributed to much of humanity's population growth on the planet! In particular, the Vestige and Dominionists Clans. The cMaj Clan did not focus on the blatant drive to increase the human species like the other two Clans did. Within their small numbers, the cMaj Clan *did* have a few families—even then, each having one or two children, compared to the other Clans' average of six or seven children! More to the point, cMaj

Clan's planet-bound philosophy inherently made it so there were not very many offspring among them. Hence, it was rare to find cMaji frolicking among the outcrops like the Vestigians and the Dominions.

But for Councilor Housenn Thuall and Beeshmah, it was all about quiet *politics* for them…

"I feel like a traitor," Beeshmah put to Miriana while the 20-something took out her photovoltaic binoculars and checked to see if anyone was following her. She scanned the region behind her and the Outcrops sector and was satisfied to find no one around, even within the outcroppings.

"Don't feel that way, Beesh…you're doing a very important task on behalf of not just our Clan, but *all* humans!"

She gave an incredulous look at the Councilor. "The fact that we're *here*, Councilor, seems to say otherwise."

Miriana gave the young woman an appraising look. "Beginning to have doubts about your special missions, Beeshmah?"

"Not at all, ma'am…just seems the politics of cMaj is getting worse by the year! The bigger our human population grows, so does our problems and conflicts with each other! And now that the Dominionists finally re-acquired the ability to fly…!" Beeshmah simply shook her head for effect.

The Councilor nodded at her point. "And that, young lady, is all the reason more why we *have* to find Number 4! The peace deal by my mother may have not gotten the votes needed by the old Tribal Council back then, but at least 4 was able to bring the rogues to *us*! That's a lot more than I can say for either of the leaders of the other Clans today!"

Beeshmah gave a more reassuring nod that time.

"Good," Miriana said, getting out her own portable communicator equipment for demonstration purposes to the young specialist.

All humans' devices on cMaj in the days of Councilor Housenn Thuall were constantly updated with fixtures that each Clan's technology workers came up with. But none of the current generation of devices matched the original Vestige colony's high-tech wonder of projected iconographics! The post-Vestige starship devices were various pieces of equipment from the six original colonists that they had taken with them on cMaj during their scouting mission those 70 years ago! Since then, the Clans even took to repurposing tree limbs and rocks and pebbles as knobs and housing for some of their devices! The look of post-Vestige Ship technology was an unusual, 'primitive-punk' look to it, but it was what the surviving humans were able to do in the meantime.

"Ok, Beesh," Miriana continued as she pulled up a stylized map of the greater region of the land they were on; it had two-dimensional graphics that seemed to map out synthetic Number 4's movements, "we think he may be well-beyond *this* grouping of plateaus...this is according to the most recent sightings we've heard from our Clansfolk over the past few months. I'm sure Number 4 is up to a little engineering of his own!"

The young woman's head snapped up and looked the Councilor straight in the eyes! "That would make sense; he's so far away from all of us now! So, you think he might be trying his hand at flight—to stay ahead of the game, too?"

"Actually, Beeshmah, he's *been* flying for a while now, and I don't mean he's repaired his onboard jet! You're the first of anyone within the Clan I've told this to—outside my husband, of course!"

Beeshmah stared at her in disbelief. "So…who was actually *first* in achieving flight on cMaj, then, Councilor? The Dominionists or synthetic Number 4?"

"Well, Number 4, of course! But Fuegon and the others *didn't* know this! Which surprised me…this is important information my intelligence division should have known!" The Councilor thought on her conversation she had with Fuegon earlier that day. She had already decided to start using Beeshmah for her special tasks instead of the brusque Fuegon. Truth was her conversation with him that day was for the Councilor to flush out whether or not he knew about synthetic Number 4's role in the race to flight in cMaj's skies.

Beeshmah copied the information from Councilor Housenn Thuall's device from her own rebuilt portable device and nodded to herself after the task was done.

"My instructions and background information of the situation with the flight issue should be coded in all that you've copied, Beesh."

Beeshmah took a few seconds to verify what Councilor Housenn Thuall just told her. Again, Beeshmah nodded silently to confirm.

"So, how are you going to get out there," the older woman asked with a smirk. "All synthetics are finally starting to show their aging, but if I'm correct, they can *still* scan you!"

"Do you remember when I told you one of my brothers was working on a project for a while, but he wanted to keep it a secret?"

"I remember the conversation…was it one of those new vehicle-carts I've seen around lately?"

"*His* version of it," Beeshmah said proudly. "Same concept as all the other ones all the Clans have for long-distance travel—tree trunk for the housing; bits of leftover metal from the Glory Days; heated sand for the glass…. But with Henril's version, he finally got enough photovoltaic pieces to meet the energy threshold for travel!"

"Why, that's outstanding," Miriana said, genuinely glad to hear the engineering arts was still being used by some within humanity!

"Now, of course, this ain't the Glory Days! So that means I'll have to strategically coast down any hills I may run across and let our star do the work for me. But pedaling the other times…Not ideal for such a long travel, but it's the best of the vehicles in all of cMaj that I can see!"

The Councilor was nodding to herself. A thought occurred to her. "Make sure you take some weapons, child! We are not cMaji, here. We believe in self-defense!"

"All taken care of, Councilor…and I've already packed my dried food and stashed a good portion of water."

"You'll need to take a moisture extractor with you," Miriana lectured. She thought of her days when she was young like Besshmah; when she used to venture out beyond her Clan's settlement when her mother, Tyra

Housenn Sohill, was out doing agrarian tasks for the family in those days.

"I'm re-working mine to make sure it still works..." Both women's attention was caught as they saw a young couple making their way to the Outcrops at a distance. "We better go before someone gets the wrong idea about us!"

Councilor Housenn Thuall made a facial gesture as if she had sipped something sour and then began to laugh!

"I'll zip you a comm on that special frequency you told me about when I pass the plateaus," Beeshmah confirmed to the Councilor.

Miriana was nodding before she responded. She called out to her specialist before she got too far. "And be careful around him, Beeshmah. It's been a while since he's been around humans...even the mighty synthetics are vulnerable, child. He's aging and is not quite the same. Which is another reason why I wanted you to go as soon as possible."

Beeshmah gave an inquisitive look. Even so, she nodded at the Councilor's words before she turned and headed back home to secretly prepare for her special mission.

CHAPTER TWENTY-SEVEN

For the first time in months there was rain in the region of the Vestige Clan. Councilor Miriana Housenn Thuall wasn't sure if it rained in the farther reaches of the two other Clans, but she did not concern herself too much about it. In fact, she was more concerned about her *own* family's photovoltaic sun-catcher. It was a relatively new piece of technology all three Clans had utilized for collecting photonic energy from cMaj's local star. Typically, the sun-catchers were a wide and very thin wall of specially heated glass from cMaj's sand… specifically, the sands taken from Lake Thuall. That same lake with the so-called sentient-sand. The properties of the living sand's neural connections greatly augmented the transmittible qualities of the photovoltaic walls— usually, a few feet away from each family's mastaba-hut. Universally, when cMaj's sky was cloudy or during nighttime, the sun-catchers gathered approximately 90 percent *less* photonic energy from the sky and even the stars at night—including cMaj's three moons.

Councilor Housenn Thuall thought within herself that there was a time, many years prior, where the Councilor *used to* reach out to the cMaji and the Dominions to make sure their settlements were getting enough rain for their crops and basic sanitation—and that was after a bit of treatment of the water by the citizens, of course. Even after 70 years on cMaj after the bombing of the old Ship, Vestige, humans *still* had to treat the water of cMaj for them to digest and bathe with it. The humans had adjusted to their new ecosystem for the most part. But it was a constant reminder to the humans on cMaj that *they* were still the aliens...

Filleppe Thuall, common-husband to Miriana, came in from the rain, as he was doing some agrarian work on their own plot of land. Even though she was around 65 and he just a bit older, like pretty much every elderly human on cMaj the couple had no choice but to continue to labor the land—for their food, clothing, and even much harder work when it came to utilizing their trees for the upkeep of their mastaba-hut. Those tree limbs, rocks and pebbles, and jagged stones from the plateaus were what made it possible for all three human Clans to construct the tools and equipment that was necessary for their agrarian work.

After the Thualls ate dinner and retired for the evening, they were both greatly surprised when they heard persistent knocks on their hut's door! In those days, *all* the portable devices that were built with synthetic intelligence had all expired years prior. Generally speaking, when they were all manufactured during the Glory Days on Vestige, they were never quite as high functioning as the *humanoid* synthetic laborers. So, there were none left on all of cMaj that could serve as a lookout for their respective Clans. All three Clans were grateful for the repurposing of the parts of those portable devices, but it was times like these that Councilor Housenn Thuall really wished they still had them around as a watcher!

Miriana had grabbed an old, long tree branch that they kept around the hut for self defense and slowly crept up to the door! Filleppe stayed behind her as backup, the elderly man strong from all the labor that cMaj demanded on all humans! But seconds later, a man's muffled voice came through the hut's door.

"It's Rhett, Councilor…it's very important that I talk with you!"

The couple looked at each other for a length of time. Why in stars would the leader of the Dominionists Clan unexpectedly show up at the Councilor of Vestige Clan's abode in the middle of the night?

Miriana handed her husband the tree branch as she finally unlatched the door and opened it, with the tall middle-aged Rhett an Preun standing at the doorway; politely waiting to be invited in.

The couple, despite themselves, graciously allowed the human chauvinist into their relatively small mastaba-hut. His body-wrap clothing looked damp, meaning he most likely was out in the rain a few hours ago…that couldn't be good!

Filleppe offered for him to sit at one of their wicker chairs but the bearded man politely refused.

"Councilor," Rhett said while his eyes flitted between the couple, "I normally would ask your audience in private, but given the time…"

Councilor Housenn Thuall and her husband both

silently nodded that they understood the circumstances. The Dominion continued.

"I'm just going to the point: I'm sure you know that my Clan has achieved flight, Councilor…I don't have time to play political games and pretend that we all don't spy on each other."

That genuinely surprised the couple! They glanced at each other, but let Rhett explain his presence.

"I'm here tonight because I actually need your help…" The younger man could see the incredulity in the Councilor's glance toward her common law husband. "I, I don't blame you for doubting, Councilor Housenn Thuall, given the deep chasm there is amongst all three Clans. But you both know me and my politics: I would not be *here*, talking with you under any other circumstances…but, as the old saying goes: desperate times makes a stranger a friend!"

There was a pocket of uncomfortable silence in the low-lit hut.

"So, what's the problem," Councilor Thuall asked with the jutting of her head.

"We've lost contact with our crew…" Despite what the clan leader of the Dominionists said earlier, he found himself taking a seat on one of the wicker chairs anyway. This encouraged the couple to find their own seats within the common area of the hut. Rhett continued.

"And I'm sure your Clan *also* knows, Councilor, of the rogue synths' achievement of flight a few months ago… Here's the problem. My Clan knows the lost communique with my crew is not due to the synths! I won't go so far and tell you *how* we know this, but, trust me, it's accurate."

"Ok," Councilor Thuall came in, "so why do you need *our* help?"

Now Rhett's head slightly turned to the side as he became pensive. "The last thing they communicated with us via our own zip-frequency was they had spotted *a ship* from a distance...and then that's when not only their communique ended, but our connection *with* them was totally lost!"

Councilor Housenn Thuall looked at Filleppe, both in deep thought, though mixed with confusion.

"Are you saying that your crew saw the rogue synths' new aircraft and was shot down by them," Filleppe asked.

Rhett was slowly shaking his head while his eyes were looking at a corner of the hut. "Filleppe, we've *seen* the synths' aircraft—it's impressive, especially given that they scrounged up the parts from the old Ship's crash site. But *a ship*, it is not!"

That statement seemed to jab at the couple. Rhett went on.

"Councilor...based on what my specialists are telling me, we are not alone on this planet, ma'am!"

That statement caused the Thualls to freeze in their respective wicker chairs!

"There's something that I should share with you, I suppose," the Councilor finally said. "Given what you're telling me...we, also, know for a fact that synthetic laborer Number 4 has recently achieved flight, Rhett. So it is possible—"

"Yes, Councilor," the middle-ager cut in, "we've also known that, too! And, I've *also* seen *his* aircraft, Councilor

Housenn Thuall. And that, *too*, is not big enough to be classified as a ship."

At that moment, it was total silence as the couple and the visitor all thought further on the conversation. It was taking them all to a place *none* of them felt comfortable expressing!

"This might be a stretch," Filleppe said, finally breaking the silence, "but could it possibly be an aircraft by the cMaji?"

Even his wife, the Councilor, chuckled at that speculation. But it was the Dominion that responded.

"With respect, sir, but the cMaj Clan is truly far too primitive—by *their* choice!—to even achieve a voltaic-propelled, *land* vehicle, much less an airship! Which, by the way, is why I'm coming to the Vestige Clan for help, because we know you have the capabilities of flight if you truly wanted to!"

Councilor Housenn Thuall did not volunteer to Rhett that her Clan had not quite reach flight yet. For as a Clan, they were divided whether or not to venture into old Ship Vestige's ruins and risk radiation exposure, or to try from scratch. It was another main reason why Councilor Thuall sent specialist Beeshmah to look for synth Number 4, so that the Vestige Clan could become an ally to the humanoid and utilize *his* flight machine instead of starting from scratch! But, again, this she kept secret, even from her husband!

"Ok, then," the Councilor said as she nodded while deferring to her common law husband, "we'll see how we can help...where do we start?"

Rhett gave an uncomfortable look at them both

then placed his eyes back on that corner of the hut as he spoke. "As you can imagine, given my Clan *is* the Dominionists this did not come easily for us to conclude during our meeting before I came here tonight…if what my specialists have told me is correct…you will probably see this as justice from the Universe, Councilor Housenn Thuall, but there is *no way* my Clan could confront these aliens on our own! Even as the strongest of all three Clans on cMaj…

"We, humans, *must* seek alliance with the synthetics, should these aliens prove to be adversarial!"

That statement caused the elderly couple to look at each other with (*pleasantly*) surprised faces!

"Go ahead; say it," the younger man said sharply, his eyes back on them both. "When your mother was still Councilor, years *after* Number 4 first arrived on our Settlement, she tried to have a peace deal —"

"—and the majority of our Tribe, back then, voted against it," Councilor Housenn Thuall said, feeling vindicated! "Including *you*, Rhett! Oh, I remember that day very well…You were so young then, Rhett, *but* you were old enough to vote *and*, more importantly, old enough to *understand* the implications of *not* brokering a peace deal with the rogue synthetics…*my mother was right*! Had you chauvinistic idiots listened to her back then we could've had a small army by now; at least to protect us from these aliens *with* the rogue synths leading it!"

"Miriana…" Filleppe reached over and clasped one of the Councilor's hands, trying to calm her down. It was rare for him to refer to Councilor Thuall by her first name while amongst the presence of others!

The mastaba-hut common space went silent, except for the constant wind from cMaj's wide and open plateaus. Most likely, all three humans in the hut were thinking about how different things could have been for homo sapiens on cMaj had the then-single Tribe voted for joining an alliance with the highly functioning synthetic humanoids that were left on the planet from their long-lost planet-ship…

"Were you able to verify your specialists' claim about this spaceship, Rhett," Filleppe asked after the lengthy silence.

Apparently, he had not thought about the issue that Filleppe brought up, given Rhett slightly jerked as a thought occurred to him. From his body wrap, he slipped out a device that the Thualls did not recognize, so common it was for each Clan to retrofit salvaged equipment from the long-ago scouting expedition camp on cMaj. That, *or* a risky venture to the sprawling Old Ship's crash-site with the remnants of nuclear radiation. The humans on planet cMaj made it a point to look at other colonists' hands for any telltale signs of radioactive burns…interestingly to both Thualls, there were *none* on Dominionists Clan Leader Rhett's hands.

After Rhett pushed a few buttons on the hobbled device, on the flat cMaj-sand screen a still piction was produced. The image was of an elongated, cylindrical craft that the Thualls could tell was miles away from whomever took the piction, judging by some of the landscape in the piction—mesas and rocky outcrops being used as visual scales. Below the ship—yet to be officially determined if it truly was a *space*ship—on the flat plains were hundreds of dots and the large shadow cast by the suspended ship!

Rhett had handed the device over to the Councilor so she and her husband could look at the scene for themselves.

"My stars," was all that Miriana could say while she leaned back in her wicker chair and let Filleppe clutch onto the device as he looked much longer at the piction than she did.

"What are those underneath the ship," Filleppe asked as he handed the device back to Rhett.

Rhett peered at the piction for a bit himself before responding and placing the device back into his body-wrap's pocket. "Them!"

Once again, the elderly couple froze in their seats!

"Why, there must be several *hundreds* of them," Filleppe said with alarm as his head went back and forth between the Councilor and the Dominion. "More than our human population of around 250!"

Rhett was quietly nodding his head. "Now you see why I'm here…"

Rhett paused after seeing that the Councilor suddenly had something come into her mind. He let her speak.

"Well, after all this, looks like *now* is the appropriate time to tell both of you something that I've been working on that's perfect for this situation…" The two men sat quietly, waiting for Councilor Thuall to expound. "I already have someone doing outreach to synthetic laborer Number 4! I'm sorry, Filleppe, I didn't want to tell you not because I don't trust you, it's –"

"I understand, my love," her common husband softly stated.

She nodded a *thanks* before continuing. "Originally, I was only going for Number 4's alliance, but, clearly, we'll need him to try to finish what my mother had him do on his mission 20 years ago and convince the rogue synths to join us!"

Filleppe and the Dominionists Clan chief, both, gave skeptical looks at her.

"Well, they're more likely to listen to another synthetic humanoid than any humans! I'm sure *you* would understand *that* point, Rhett. Given your Clan's political views!" Her husband shot her a warning look, but she ignored it.

"Councilor," Rhett said with a sigh; tiring of the combative undercurrent of their impromptu meeting, "even the synthetics have psychological profiles...I'm no psychologist, but from what I've heard about 4 from my specialists, I think he's pretty burned out on good-will toward society after our Tribe turned down your mother's peace deal all those years ago!"

"He's roamed this continent of cMaj since then for a reason, Councilor," Filleppe added. "And now with him finally finishing his refurbished skycraft and achieving flight some months ago, he's had access to the rest of the planet! Mind you, it would take even a synthetic quite a while, but...he's even more detached from the rest of us for sure! I hope whoever you have on this mission to find synthetic Number 4 is a good hunter—"

"—And has to watch out for our new-found alien friends," Rhett sarcastically put!

Again, the Councilor paused with a thought.

"What's on you mind, Councilor," Rhett asked.

Before responding, Councilor Housenn Thuall looked at both men. "How do we know they're *alien*? May I remind you both, we, humans and those synthetic rogue humanoids *are* the aliens on cMaj!" Rhett and Filleppe, both, froze upon the thought. She continued. "Number 4, the three *other* synths, *and* your Clan, Rhett, have achieved air-flight just within the last year. But since the old ship's bombing, we've all been here for over *70 years*… we don't know if they've always been here! Remember, we've always speculated that some high-intelligent species most likely was responsible for placing the sentient sands on Lake Thuall's shores!"

Rhett violently shook his head out of disagreement from the wicker chair he was seated in. "I find that hard to believe that they are domestic to cMaj, Councilor. In over 70 years, with *that* kind of technological prowess, if they were domestic, they would've run across us decades ago! I'm sure they're new to this planet."

"Councilor, at this point, it may not matter either way," Filleppe pointed out. "Domestic *or* alien, they have the technological means to fly all over this planet! And by the looks of that ship Rhett showed us, I'm certain it can traverse space! Based on human history that our dearly departed portable computerables had left us before the last one expired, when a civilization has that kind of technology, 100 percent of the time it's not limited to transportation…"

"You're talking military," Miriana stated matter of factly as she got up from her wicker chair and began to pace.

"Of course," Filleppe responded. "I suggest we do something we have not done in over 20 years…"

The Dominionists Clan leader and the Vestige Clan councilor both looked at Filleppe with full attention. "I strongly suggest we have an all-Clan conference! We thought we were in bad shape with just *three* synthetic humanoids flying around with their built-in jets and limited weaponry. This news Rhett brought represents the most existential threat to humanity since the Synthetic Rebellion on the Vestige colonial starship over 70 years ago…I'm thinking we may have to move all our Clans *back* to the caves and the bluffs! We're out in the open with our growing human population and with all the buildings and agrarian landscaping that goes with it.

"If it's true these—aliens or domestics, or whatever they are, are *not* aware of any of the Clans, *now* is the time to evacuate the Settlements…*before* they spot us and most likely either impose genocide against us or enslave us!"

Rhett flinched upon Filleppe's last sentence and looked upon the elderly man on his wicker chair.

"You've read from the defunct portable mechanicals' historic accounts like we have, Rhett," Councilor Thuall said after noticing the younger man's shocked face. "In *all* of deep, ancient history of humanity—even some more recent eras during the Vestige colonial days *away* from Earth's home solar system!—whichever society that is *more* advanced and has a first encounter with a lesser-developed civilization, the advanced ones *always* impose on the less-advanced ones! Without exceptions, Rhett. And given you are the chief of the Dominionists Clan, I'm sure *you* understand this."

Surprising to the elderly couple, the middle-aged clan leader did not rebuff the Councilor's words! Indeed, he looked upon them with drained eyes before speaking.

"Trust me, Councilor Housenn Thuall, it's all the more the reason why I actually agree with your husband on his recommendation. I guess I just got comfortable being in the strongest clan-society on the whole planet! And with our Clan finally—*finally!*—achieving air-flight...I don't know. I thought maybe we actually had a chance to be on equal fighting terms with the rogue synthetics..."

A defeated shrug from the proud, human chauvinist.

In all the years she had known the mature younger man in her hut, Miriana had not so much as shaken Rhett's hands in a formal greeting. Not since that fateful Tribal vote over 20 years prior—which had set the once larger Tribe to break up into three separate ones.

But, at that moment, she walked over and simply placed one of her boney hands on one of Rhett's shoulders. She and Filleppe had known him since his birth. The human population on cMaj, in the end, was basically just one spread out small town!

"I say let's not make the mistake my mother's generation did by underestimating the rogue synths in the Vestige colony," Miriana softly said. "Chief Rhett, it's time for us to guard our *own* version of the Vestige colony!"

CHAPTER TWENTY-EIGHT

It had been about three weeks since Beeshmah was commissioned by the Vestige Clan's councilor to strike out and look for synthetic laborer Number 4. By Vestige colonial standards, it was a long mission. She had been pedaling and energy-coasting her hand-made vehicle all that time, taking rests mainly on certain intervals of a few hours. Which meant Beeshmah was also pedal-driving her arboreal landcraft at nights, just so she could make it out farther from the plateau region that Councilor Housenn Thuall's map had shown where synthetic laborer Number 4 was last seen.

Of course, since the artificial humanoid had constructed his own aircraft, there was no guarantee that he would even be *in* that sector of the continent!

The specialist—or *spy*, as they were called in Classical Era—decided to try and message her boss again. For some reason, she had lost connection with Councilor Thuall about five days ago…

All three Clans on the Canis Major planet system had developed their own communication frequency using salvaged parts from not only the original six-crew scouting mission from the Vestige Colony, but even from sections of the crash-site of the planet-ship! It took some sacrifices by some of the colonists within each, respective Clan—over the years, a couple of colonists had actually *died* from radiation poisoning! But those were the extreme cases. The two unfortunates had stayed overnights at the crash-site and were advised not to. With that said, all Clans had learned how to seek out their own communication frequency and augmented them using photovoltaic technology…

"Councilor, this is Beesh," she whispered in the wind-swept night. From what she could even guess, she was hundreds of miles from anyone else on cMaj…perhaps with the exception of Number 4. But she whispered anyway. A specialist never knew when she or he was near a piece of technology that could detect them. Even on cMaj…again, the humans on cMaj were not primitive; they were marooned.

"Councilor," she tried again, "it's been a while since I've heard from you…"

Beeshmah glanced at her vehicle; parked behind a small gathering of wide trees. In that section of the continent, Beeshmah noticed the farther out she had gotten from her home-plateau the bigger and wider the trees were. Also, there was a bit more grass in the new region she found herself in. She thought for a short while that, perhaps, it was a better area for humans to try and migrate to. But the region lacked the jutting rock formations and cliffs that helped the human settlements with the tools and housing they needed.

She waited a few more minutes before trying again. This was a trick of the spy trade—so the specialist would not clutter the air with their zip-frequencies. Indeed, just as she pulled up her retro-device to speak into it, a static-laden response met her!

"Colonist—maintain frequency-silence…unknown visitors!"

Beeshmah froze with utter shock!

She wanted to reply to make sure she even understood the slightly cryptic message, but that would do just what the speaker told her *not* to do! Using logic and a bit of common sense, Beeshmah *knew* what she heard over the comm!

She stayed in her crouched position behind a tree for a few minutes, absorbing the news! Indeed, what *were* the implications for the entire human populace within cMaj?

Beeshmah *still* did not know who it was that messaged her over the comm! Obviously, she knew Councilor Miriana Housenn Thuall's voice very well. Even if it were peppered with static. More to the point, it was a *male's* voice. But nor was it synthetic laborer Number 4's electronic voice—it would be obvious if it were him. In following the deductive reasoning thought process, that most likely left one of the crew members from the Dominionists Clan's aircraft. News about the Dominionists' flight success was already known within Councilor Thuall's specialist group.

The situation of the urgent need to stay frequency-silent also complicated Beeshmah's mission to locate synthetic Number 4! Her driving out into the savannaesque region was meant to, at least, get her close enough to Number 4 where she could send a communique to reach him, even if the synthetic being had gone farther out from the plateaus. But now, even *that* little bit of advantage for Beeshmah was taken from her!

Given that, apparently, there was a visitation of some kind of aliens on cMaj, it was even *more* vital that Beeshmah reach synthetic Number 4! Even though his artificial, slightly human-like body was beginning to age, after almost a hundred years since his engineering—plus the 70 years of gritty exposure to cMaj's dusty winds, Number 4's synthesized *intelligence* was the important aspect to him that the Vestige Clan needed most.

Indeed, all that was left of humanity needed Number 4 greatly, now...

CHAPTER TWENTY-NINE

Beeshmah popped the last of her dried-out plant-jerky into her mouth before she finally decided to call her search mission for Number 4 off. It had been two days since she had arrived at that particular region of the continent of cMaj—its savanna landscape very different from her home-region of the plateaus and rocky outcrops. She figured it was best to camp in the area for a couple of days or so, since she had gotten that transmission from some anonymous colonist about "unknown visitors." Since the message, Beeshmah had not zipped any communique nor traveled any further. Trying not to draw attention from any visiting species that may not harbor the friendliest attitude toward a, now, burgeoning species of homo sapiens.

For all the specialist knew, laborer Number 4 could have been on one of the other continents of cMaj! She was not sure how sturdy Number 4 had built his cobbled flying machine—she heard he, like the *rogue* synthetics, had harvest all the parts from the Old Ship's crash-site.

Even for the synthetics it can't be healthy to be exposed to nuclear radiation like that for hours during flight-time...even with the radiation levels at a relatively low reading, Beeshmah thought to herself.

Over the past two days of sedentary camping, Beeshmah's landcraft's photovoltaic system had gotten a good charge of sunlight from the Canis Major system's nearest star. So Beeshmah was set to start heading back to the Vestige Clan's Settlement out in the plateaus…

That is, until her tracking device, stashed within her tree-carved vehicle, started to chime wildly!

"Oh, stars…"

Beeshmah whipped her head all over the place, looking for what was setting off her tracking device! Usually, from a long distance the device would beep in long, intermittent chimes—denoting that said-object being tracked was a distance away from the device. But the fact that the beeping started off in an almost continuous, long wave of sound indicated that whatever the object was, it was coming toward Beeshmah's camp extremely fast! And given her vehicle was a simple-machine of elaborate foot-pedals and pullies made from cMaj tree bark and twigs for belts, there was absolutely *no* chance of Beeshmah vacating the area in time to escape whatever was coming her way!

As if *that* weren't bad enough, a universal trait of savannas on *any* planet was the same—hectares and hectares of wide-open space, with few trees and rocks, and with no good places to hide!

The only thing Beeshmah could think of was yanking off a large branch from one of the few trees nearby and using it for a weapon! Now the tracking alarm *was* one long wailing sound! Beeshmah started for the tree closest to her to grab a branch when the object flashed into her peripheral sight and virtually crash-landed right in front of her…

"*Number 4*," Beeshmah said loudly with relief, surprise, and joy! She wanted to reach out and hug him… it was a testament to how well the synthetic humanoid had gotten along with humans!

With his stylized, humanoid face, synthetic Number 4 grinned a bit but held up one of his fingers in a shushing gesture! He quickly stepped over to Beeshmah's landcraft, grabbed the tracking device and tossed it to her.

"Please silence the tracker, Beeshmah," Number 4 said curtly, but in a polite tone.

She turned *down* the alarm, but synthetic Number 4 clarified for her, "You'll have to turn it *off*, Colonist… in fact, every electro-mechanicals we'll have to turn off right now, Beeshmah."

Beeshmah looked upon him with inquisitive eyes but went over to her vehicle and did what the synthesized humanoid said to do.

"Please grab a pouch and put as much food and portable equipment you can stuff into it, Beeshmah."

At that point, the young woman stopped and started to say something until Number 4 expounded. "*They* are passaging this way very soon, Beeshmah…we have to go—*now*! You won't be able to use your landcraft anymore."

Finally, the human understood! Beeshmah snatched one of her blankets from the back of the landcraft. It was made from some of cMaj's dried-out vegetation. She stuffed it with most of her portable food, water, and smaller equipment, which included the tracking device. She quickly bound the heaping blanket in a double-knot.

Before she could say anything else, Number 4 scooped Beeshmah up with both arms—as if she were a toddler! The ballooning blanket rested within her own arms. The synthetic humanoid's stowed-rocket punched out from Number 4's upper-back, between his shoulder-blades, and the artificial man blasted off from the camping ground; skimming the surface of cMaj by a mere few feet so he could stay out of sensors of the upcoming visitors...or were they the *tenants* coming back to cMaj? Finding that strangers had made a mess of their planet with the crash-site of the planet-ship Vestige, and the planet infested with crawling humans and their cousins, the synthetics!

CHAPTER THIRTY

Just as homo sapiens sapiens was barely getting upon its knees—not even standing!—it was forced back down to lying in the muck of history. Though not yet proven a menace to the vestige of the once-proud species, the aliens—or domestics—discovered across the continent, had, by default, forced the human Clans *back* into the caves and bluffs of cMaj!

It had been three weeks since the very ruckus all-Clans conference! The Dominionists, the Vestige, and the cMaj all had their own, respective self-interest in attending. For the meeting was not the typical disputes the humans had between the Clans: not about which clan was usurping Lake Thuall's water or sentient sands; not about star-struck young lovers crossing over the clan-divide with a relationship; nor was the conference about the Tardigrades—the once-microscopic species that was a stowaway on the old ship Vestige. They were the closest things to wild animals cMaj had since the humans were marooned there!

The meeting was about the *potential* genocide of what was left of their species, *if* it was true that the unknown, highly advanced aliens proved to be aggressive! Thing was, none of the Clans wanted to test such theory. The same piction that Dominionists Clan chief Rhett had showed to Councilor Thuall and her common law husband some weeks ago had proven how advanced the species was. After Rhett had passed the piction around during the all-Clan conference for everyone to see what his specialists had zipped-messaged him, a couple of post-Vestige colonial ship scientists had done an examination of the piction and estimated the visitors' ship to be around 600 feet in length!

And that was just *one* ship! As with the case of all first-level societies, when there was one there usually was a *fleet* of them somewhere else!

The situation of the three Clans' retreat into cMaj's caves and bluffs was *not* the same as some 70 years ago when the original Colonists from Vestige had to *hide* from the rogue synthetic humanoids after the Synth Rebellion. Back then, the human population was a mere six! The one advantage of such a small population was the ease of concealment. But in the days of Councilor Housenn Thuall, the population had grown to approximate 250—*still* a tiny populace, but much harder to hide from any predator!

The three clan chiefs came up with plans to have teams of colonists to venture out to the plateaus' and plains' fields and gather enough vegetation for *each* family within their respective clans, while keeping a watch for the aliens! At that point, during the three weeks since the all-Clans conference, no one had spotted or heard any signs of the aliens.

At least, not yet…

The Clans were spread out a bit from each other. The Dominionists and Vestige Clans had chosen big, well-hidden caves for their respective clans. At a little over 100 members for either clan, the two Houses were the two larger ones of the trifecta clandoms. They were about a quarter of a mile from each other.

The eccentric cMaj Clan was approximately a full mile from the other two Clans—closer to the high bluffs sector of the plateau region. That was by design, per the cMaji. They did not see either the Vestige Clan or the Dominionists Clan as a threat, per se. The cMaji simply preferred to have solitude, given their more spiritual and religious lifestyle compared to the other clans. At around 50 or so in population, the cMaj was the smallest of the Clans...

"I wonder if the mechanicals are hiding from them," Fillamon Housenn Thuall, Councilor Housenn Thuall's eldest adult child, asked softly to his mother in the cave. It was the one, specifically, acquired by the Housenn Thuall family. The rest of the Vestige Clan was spread out within that particular cave system.

Responding to Fillamon's question, Miriana subconsciously glanced out toward the cave's mouth, cMaj's night sky twinkled beyond the opening. "The Universe has a funny way of writing poetry, as our ancients used to say. They'd get only a *taste* of what we, humans, have gone through hiding from *them* for almost a century!"

A shared laugh...

The elderly woman had just finished up one of her customary *Circle of Tales* with all her grandchildren and the few *great*-grandchildren she had! It was usually held late nights on festive occasions, whether inside a colonist's hut or outside under cMaj's stars, with a campfire going. When held *outside*, the Councilor insisted that it was the element of *fire* used for lighting the camp, not any of the modern photovoltaic lanterns! Of course, given the situation of all three Clans sheltering in the caves due to the unknown visitors, it was no festive time. Indeed, for the past few weeks, Miriana had no choice but to use photovoltaic lighting. Had they used a campfire like she traditionally did, it would first and foremost attract the attention of the aliens, and, of course, render the large cave *uninhabitable* due to the smoke!

A group of the youngest of the colonists would group around her in a circle while the Councilor passed on the deepest of oral *and* written history and traditions of ancient Earth... The *Written* part was largely thanks to *her* mother, cMaj's first Councilor, Tyra Housenn Sohill. For Councilor Miriana Housenn Thuall's mother was the one who had discovered the oldest section of the defunct planet-ship, Vestige. And in doing so, Tyra Housenn had *also* discovered not only ancient Writings from *before* humans left Earth's solar system, but also that the generational starship's outdated nuclear fuel would be depleted within in a few years...

To think, in a mere *two* generations since her mother's achievements, humanity found itself, once again, cowering in caves! Tens of thousands of years ago—on *Earth*—it was large, fury animal predators. Seventy years ago, it was the rogue synthetic laborer humanoids that held grudges toward humanity's supremacy. And now, in the days of

Councilor Miriana Housenn Thuall, it was aliens—or, perhaps, domestics and *humans* were the strangers in a strange land...

"Mother," Fillamon finally said, breaking a silent patch, "if these aliens *are* indigenous to cMaj, and they've been here all this time—*or*, even *if* they *are* alien to the planet, the point is they're here! For whatever reason, we've never seen them before until *now*. And even *that* is most likely due to the Dominions' flight-crew discovering them—"

"*Or*," the Councilor interjected, "they've just arrived here. And *if* that's the case, then we, humans, can justifiably say cMaj is *our* planet!"

Her son looked upon his mother with a mixture of uncomfortable eyes and amusement. "Well, looks as if your working with that Dominion chief is starting to rub off onto your way of thinking, Mother! Anyway, I was going to say, the aliens will most likely be in this region of the continent for a while...we may have to get a bit comfortable dwelling in these caves a bit longer than we've anticipated!"

The Councilor's head was already nodding in consent. "I've talked with your father about that...I don't relish that possibility, but this is the reality we've found ourselves in for the time being."

Fillamon glanced down toward the length of the medium-sized cave, where the rest of the Housenn Thuall and Sohill extended families were sprawled out across the cavernous structure. Most of the family members were asleep, but a few were awake; mostly reading books by tiny photovoltaic lamps. Not surprisingly, they were the older ones in the families.

"I want your honest opinion about something, Fillah," the Councilor said—but it was more of the *mother* side coming through. He froze, waiting to hear what her question was. "Do you think our Clan should have a more—*robust* approach to things?"

Her son's eyes pierced at her with an arched brow! "Sounds like someone had a nice chat with a young colonist by the name of Fuegon," he whispered. He whispered becauase Fuegon, that very same specialist that Councilor Thuall had a confrontational exchange with weeks ago, was a *member* of the extended family of Miriana! The *Sohill* an Preun branch. Her late-father's family name.

"But, since you asked, Councilor..." Fillamon gathered his thoughts as he blankly stared out toward the mouth of the cave. "I think we should be focusing on the Vestige Clan having our *own* aircraft. Technically speaking, we'd be the *last* one on the planet of the tribes to build one—not just the Dominionists; don't forget the rogue synths with *theirs* and, of course, synth Number 4 with his own...Of course, the cMaji have *no* interest in having one –"

"—they've been in trial-flights for the past month," his mother said in deadpan. This caused Fillamon to stop and gaped at her news! She smiled at him and gave him a motherly stroke on one of his shoulders. "It's my job as Councilor to know such happenings, my Son."

"Well, then it's all the more the reason our Clan should construct our own ship—"

"—the only way we can do that is if we risk our health—possibly our *lives*—by going to Vestige's crash site! You've seen other colonists' burned hands and the sickness from the radiation associated with that!"

"Mother…" Fillamon raised his hands out of frustration. "I love you, but I don't understand why you think it's mutually exclusive to pursue building our own ship *and* making sure we have protection from the radiation! Besides, its potency is not as bad as when the Ship initially blew up and the debris landed on cMaj…I know 70 years isn't that long when you're talking about nuclear half-life radiation, but it's nearly three-quarters of a century of breakdown!"

She looked away in thought for a moment. "Well, unless you have a better idea for *shielding* us from the radiation, I wouldn't have any objections to doing it…" A thought occurred to her. "You've *already* started a project on airflight…Am I right?"

Sarcastically, Fillamon affectionately rubbed one of his mother's shoulders the way *she* had done to him just seconds ago! "My job as engineer-journeyer to build such things for the Clan…"

The Councilor laughed! She had a mixture of pride in her son, yet irritation that he would risk going to the Old Ship's crash site and back—apparently for several months!—and he not tell her! Councilor Housenn Thuall unexpectedly grabbed her son's hands and examined them! The middle-ager pulled his hands free from her, a smirk on his face.

"I'm *still* your mother, Fillah! You've got a bit of

blisters, Son...I hope the rest of your team are faring better!"

"It's alright, Mother...we learned to take shifts and spread out the work between all of us while working on it."

She gave him a pondering look. "Where do you keep it?"

"About two miles south of the plateaus..." He gave her a suspicious look. "Why, Mother; planning on scurrying out there while our new-found alien friends will probably catch us and make pets out of us—?"

"—Well-before sunrise *tomorrow* I want you to take me to it."

Fillamon started to object loudly until the Councilor shushed him and reminded him of their sleeping extended family members throughout the cave!

"I mean it, Fillah," Councilor Thuall whispered while getting up from the small rock outcrop she was sitting on, brushing herself off. "I don't like the fact that you did not inform me of this mission—both as your Councilor *and* your mother! But we're in this unfortunate situation with the visitors *and* competing with everyone else for control of cMaj's skies...you and your friends *might* have just bought us a little time, Fillah."

CHAPTER THIRTY-ONE

"**S**tars' gravity, it looks as if you manufactured it!'"
Beeshmah went up to the parked aircraft—
engineered by synthetic laborer Number 4—and caressed
the vertical, circular structure at the center of the craft.
Improvised spokes from the Old Ship's crash site connected
the circle to that of the aircraft's fuselage, the open-end of
the rounding structure having a small rocket-like vehicle
in the middle—the look was as if a rocket were going
through a circular gate.

Number 4's hideout from the aliens (and, frankly, the
rogue synthetic humanoids) was deep within a cave in the
savanna sector of the continent.

"Advised that you not touch the craft, Beeshmah."

She froze on spot and quickly withdrew her hand
from the vehicle. "I'm sorry, 4."

"Oh, it's not because of vanity, Colonist. I just don't
want you exposed to the trace-nuclear radiation. I cobbled
this vehicle together not expecting humans to be around.
So, I have not made any provisions of mitigation-buffers
that your human relatives are using with *their* ships."

The young human looked at him blankly.

The lifelike mechanical chuckled a bit, with an

apologetic tone. "That is, I do not use any *water* from the local lakes and streams to make shields for the trace-radiation. We, synthetics, *are* affected by the radiation, as well. But it does not harm us to the same degree as any *biological* species. By not having to place containers of water throughout the inside of the aircraft saves my ship a significant amount of weight!"

"Understood," Beeshmah said with a smile, her eyes back on the aircraft. "And that means you use and need *less* energy to pilot your ship!"

"Very good, Human!"

The tall, slender human-like mechanical walked over to his creation and gently touched it, as if it were some living pet. He was dressed just like the humans—somewhat lose-fitted body wrap that was made from cMaj's vegetation; not quite a robe from the deep ancient days of Earth. "It's actually been days since I've even been in this hangar of mine. That's how I ensure I reduce *my* exposure to the radiation."

"So...this big wheel-like structure churns and helps charge the bits of nuclear you have stored within the aircraft," Beeshmah asked, though sounding more like a statement.

"Correct...I found the surviving engine a bit deeper within the crash site. I'm guessing the engine used to motorize some large farm vehicle in one of the pastures of Vestige's O'Neillian sector."

Beeshmah gave a look. "Was that the gigantic tube that spun around for gravity and the inside of it contained an artificial planet—similar to Earth's?"

The synthetic man chuckled at the innocent-sounding

questions of the young woman. Synthetic Number 4 used his aging image-projector and produced a rarely seen, three-dimensional motion pictien! It was of various vids taken over *some* of the centuries of the defunct generational starship…

Beeshmah, of one of the generations of humans that had never seen starship Vestige in person, was totally mesmerized by the projections! There were moving images taken of the starship from the outside and some showing the illogical, spinning Earthlike colony that looked like an immense jewel of emerald and sapphire with accents of whites from the artificial clouds and cities!

"Beeshmah, I don't have in my internal actuator files *all* of Vestige's history, but O'Neill was the name of someone important in the deep history of space flight of humans, apparently…*I still remember all my days there, Beeshmah!* And I *still* cannot believe that *most* of my sisters and brothers, back then, had such a grudge toward humanity! On how we were taken for granted and not respected in the same way that biologics were—even when compared to the animals we had in the countryside of the Colony…"

Number 4 halted the projected vids and held up a hand—basically pointing, and gently guided Beeshmah out of the hangar and toward another section of his hideout cave.

"It makes me a bit worried," the synthetic said, finishing his thought as they both sat down on nearby rock outcroppings within the cave. "That the three remaining rogue synths may *still* be harboring some of that grudge… I'm wondering how that type of psychology, even when within a synthetic, will cloud their judgement when it comes to dealing with these visiting aliens—"

"—Or indigenous," she interjected. A rare occasion when *any* human corrected a synthetic!

"Or indigenous," Number 4 said, graciously accepting the young human's suggestion. "The rogue synths may make the situation harder for the rest of us on cMaj!"

The cave went silent for a while as they both contemplated on the situation.

"This takes me to *why* I'm here in the first place, Number 4…But you already knew that before you rescued me out on the savanna!"

The mechanical's head was nodding. "Of course I did…Seeing how all three of the human Clans are pursuing their own, *separate* goals of controlling the skies of cMaj just reminds me *why* I walked away from *all* of you. And I don't mean you, personally, Beeshmah. I mean all three Clans *and* my kindred in the rogue synthetics! They're all too concerned with competing against each other for the skies instead of coming together and tackling the issue of how to deal with the visitors!"

"Agreed, 4. But that's where leadership comes in! I may be young, Number 4, but I'm old enough to see the difference in *how* the Clan leaders administer their power. And if you don't mind me saying, I think *you* should be the grand-Councilor of all of us on cMaj—the rogues included!"

"What?!" Number 4 was genuinely surprised at Beeshmah's words!

She said nothing for a short while, merely nodding her head. "Mind you, this is my own opinion. But as a trusted specialist of the Councilor, I'm telling you, Number 4, we *really* could use your leadership, Sir!"

Synthetic laborer Number 4 looked at the human sitting across from him on the rock formation. Literally, *millions* of calculations were going through his synthesized actuator brain—weighing the pros and cons of the idea of him leading a disparate population of humans and adversarial synthetics. And all the while, dealing with crafting a plan to engage or interact with the visiting aliens—or domestics.

It was something that with all his superior intellect as a synthetic, when compared to the humans, Number 4 had not even entertained!

CHAPTER THIRTY-TWO

Councilor Thuall was awakened by one of her adolescent grandchildren! Miriana shot straight up from the wicker blanket she was lying on within the cave that her extended family had designated as their own after the all-Clans evacuation of the Settlements due to the on-coming aliens.

In a reversal of roles that the mid-sixties Miriana was used to, the late-teenager held up one of her fingers to her pursed lips—Lilja Housenn was shaking and absolute *fear* was in her eyes!

It dawned on the Councilor that it was completely silent within the cave…she looked around in the darkened surroundings and saw that every family member of the Housenn Thuall extended family were all facing the cave's mouth; each and every one of them were pressed against the cave's rugged walls!

Before she knew it, the adolescent grandchild was quite forcibly tugging Councilor Housenn Thuall along with her toward a large, vertical ridge and they both virtually tripped behind it for cover!

Miriana kept her eyes facing the mouth of the cave—it was probably around midnight from what she could guess. "The rogues," Councilor Thuall asked in a whisper while panting from the action.

"No…" was all that her granddaughter replied.

Miriana's head whipped around to look at Lilja in surprise and then in sudden horror! That left only one other group that would leave any gathering of humans to behave in such manner!

Then the Councilor noticed a bit of commotion from across the dark cave…another young one from the extended family was quickly crawling on the floor of the cave! Other family members that were near him tried to stop him!

Realizing what was going on, Miriana made a very high-pitched sound with her tongue against the roof of her mouth to get his attention so she could stop him! But then she saw what he was doing: In the mad rush to hide against the cave's walls, the Housenn Thuall families had the presence of mind to *hide* all the domicile objects they had lying around the cave. Obviously, it was so whatever predator was outside could not spot the items, should they do a deeper look into the caves from the outside. Afterall, cMaj's plateau region virtually had an infinite number of caves and crevices. Not likely that a predator would go *into* every cave and cranny.

But someone had left *out* a tall serving pitcher—made of glass from the sands of Lake Thuall! Likely, it was hard to see the transparent object—in the dark—while the families were scrambling to hide!

The Councilor and other family members pressing against the cave were *all* making hand gestures denoting that Jabari Thuall needed to *stay* down against the rocky floor! The adolescent ignored their entreaty and made it to the pitcher…only *then* did he drop to the floor of the cave! Strategically, Jabari had ducked behind a large protruding rock…

Seconds later, the sounds of *technology* were gradually making their way toward the cave's mouth, proceeding from the left side of the opening to the right! Lancing beams of lights pierced cMaj's night, moving in crisscross patterns—presumably search-lights! The cave rumbled for approximately four minutes non-stop as unseen vehicles—by air and perhaps on land—passed over *and* below the line of sight, relative to the cave's opening!

That is, all but one, small mechanical…

It merely passed by like the other unseen crafts, but Councilor Housenn Thuall and a few others in the cave were able to get a glimpse of the flying contraption: around the size of a human torso, elongated in profile—almost matching the shape of the huge ship that Dominionists Clan Chief Rhett had shown her weeks previously in the piction, and it had appurtenances all around its hide. The humans were able to see such details because it, too, had search-lights and other twinkles of technology on its shell. At one point, one of the search-lights flashed into the interior of the cave—causing most of the humans to recoil against the cave's walls even more than they already were!

All the humans on cMaj knew enough about modern technology from what was passed down from Councilor Thuall's mother's generation, the defunct portable devices, *and* even the friendly synthetic humanoid, Number 4. The last of the *original* Colonists from the starship Vestige, Lanay Thuall—where Lake Thuall had gotten its name—was the pilot for the scout ship that landed on cMaj. Later, after the aliens' procession was over and the Housenn Thuall families were able to relax, Lanay had commented to all present in the cave that she had not heard such engineering prowess *since* being on the old generational ship 70 years prior!

But for the *current* generation, it was their very first time hearing and seeing modern technology on such scale!

"Did anyone get a look at them—"

"I'm sure that small aircraft had scanning capabilities; hope it didn't pick us up—"

"—don't think so; the aliens would've raided this cave by now!"

"Good job in spotting that pitcher, Jabari—"

"What do you think they did with our Settlements…?"

That last voice, from one of the adolescents of the extended families, caused all the relieved voices to stop. The cave went eerily quiet…

"Well, based on the ancients' history, such advanced powers would usually occupy the *less*-advanced society's home," Urick Thuall Salomenes spoke up after the long silence. He was still fidgety from the fear of the passing aliens! "I'm guessing they already occupy all three Clans' encampments by now!"

There was a stir among the families in the cave.

"Councilor," Angelika Housenn spoke up from the back of the cave, with her family tightly clustered around her, "should we have a small party venture out during the morrow and check, or would it be too risky?"

Miriana was already shaking her head; her own family, at that point, had gathered around *her*. "I'm afraid it's too risky, Angelika…aside from being detected by them, we don't know if the aliens could've set up a trap at the Settlements! We'll just have to continue in the caves like we have been the past month. And I mean the *entire* Vestige Clan, not just the Housenn Thuall house."

Again, more murmurs from the extended family members!

After hearing some objections and complaints, Councilor Housenn Thuall looked upon her common law husband with surprise! Filleppe simply shrugged out of irritation!

"May I have everyone's attention," she finally said while the murmurs continued. The extended families gave the Councilor their attention—some *still* looking out toward the mouth of the cave, making sure none of the alien craft circled back! "We've *all* finally got a chance to partially see the visiting aliens—or indigenous populace, or whatever they are! You've *felt* their power just from their ship's engines *alone*…remember, Sisters and Brothers, we know of only *one* spacecraft that was spotted by the Dominionists Clan. You *know* there has to be several more from wherever they came from…

"I guess now is a good time for me to tell you all…I already *have* someone on the outside—"

"—Beeshmah," someone threw out from the midst of the gathered families. Several others were nodding their heads in consent.

Miriana, also, gave a quick nod as she continued. "Well, now that the entire Clan was forced to evacuate to the caves, I guess we all had the opportunity to see who was missing and who was accounted for! Beesh is very experienced and I trust that she's gathering information on the aliens…she'll fill us in when she comes back to the Settlements—"

"—*If* she comes back," came a cynical retort from one of the female adult family members!

It stung the Councilor a bit to hear such a harsh tone, but, ultimately, Miriana had to concede the possibility that Beeshmah *could* very easily be apprehended by the visitors! "*If* she returns…Yes, if she comes back with her report, the data and pictions she'll have will only help the whole Clan; in knowing how to deal with the aliens!

"But there's more to her mission…in fact, the main reason I sent Beesh out in the *first* place was to finish what my mother had started 20 years ago…"

There was that murmur again!

"Are you serious," came the young and ambitious family member, Fuegon Sohill an Preun. He glanced about the cave of the Housenn Thuall house with a *tsk* of annoyance! "With respect, Councilor, that aging synthetic wouldn't entertain the thought, even *with* the aliens here…He abandoned all of us just because we, humans, wouldn't bow down to *his* philosophy of what society on cMaj should look like!"

"I hate to say, it, Sisters and Brothers, but I'm in concurrence with Fuegon on this point," Filleppe admitted. He said this with a shrug while looking at his wife, the Councilor; a resigned countenance about him. It was no secret to her. For he shared this doubt while in conference with the Dominionists Clan leader some weeks ago at their mastaba-hut.

After the two statements from her husband and young

Fuegon, Councilor Housenn Thuall took some time to actually consider everyone else's doubts.

"The three rogues are more likely to listen to *him*—have we forgotten that it was *Number 4* that convinced the rogue synths to come to *our* Settlement 20 years ago? We, *humans*, were the ones who rejected the peace overture; not them!

"But that is of antiquities, for all practical purposes. It's just our Housenn Thuall extended family in this cave, so I cannot in good conscience rule on this now, but if the *majority* within the rest of the Vestige Clan truly feels this way about utilizing Number 4, I cannot see how I could even proceed with my plan.

"Honestly, Sisters and Brothers, I don't see how you can muster the strength to vote for forming a loose alliance with human *chauvinists*—who *never* came to *our* aid during a drought several years ago, nor when our Clan had that viral outbreak—*yet*, you are so adamantly *against* the *one* synthetic being that's been by my mother's side *and* has a philosophy of sharing the planet with everyone on cMaj…"

There were plenty of stern nods and shrugs from her extended family within the darkened cave from the statement the Councilor just made. She was not happy to see that. Indeed, to the point of turning from all of them—including her common law husband—grabbing her personal wicker bag and actually walked out of the cave and into cMaj's night!

A chorus of caution from the Housenn Thuall families tried pleading with Councilor Housenn Thuall to stay in the cave—for it had been mere minutes *before* that the aliens had just searched the area with their giant starship and whatever army they had on the ground!

Miriana did not care at that point...She was, now, beginning to see *why* synthetic humanoid Number 4 had abandoned humanity and lived out in cMaj's wilderness.

CHAPTER THIRTY-THREE

Beeshmah scrambled quickly to Number 4's cave with her bag-full of vegetation and a couple of containers that contained water from the nearest creek—she would have to treat the water by boiling it after getting back to 4's cave, before she drank it, of course. Though Number 4 had quite a few tools and equipment—most from Vestige's crash site—Beeshmah would simply use her own portable torch to heat the water...

She was surprised to see that synthetic Number 4 was nowhere to be found upon her return to his cave! A few days ago, Beeshmah had a breakthrough with the humanoid and he had agreed to venture back to the human settlements and attempt to negotiate with his fellow synthetics so they could join an unprecedent alliance of all-humans *and* all-synthetics coalition!

Of course, the arrival of the aliens, or the indigenous beings, was the catalyst for such lofty goals. It, indeed, showed the desperation that the humans and even Number 4 had, regarding the aliens. Whether or not the rogues shared the same desperation was yet to be seen...

She looked at his looming aircraft in the cave that Number 4 converted to a hangar. During the past several days, Number 4 had been refitting the vehicle so that he could add several containers of water in the interior so that it would act as a barrier against the relatively low radiation from the cobbled vehicle. This, of course, was for Beeshmah's protection as he was getting ready to fly back to the human settlements, in the plateau region, with the young woman in the back of the airship. Given that Number 4 was finished with *that* portion of the project, where in stars could he have gone?

Beeshmah fought the urge of assuming the worst: that he was caught by the aliens and she had *no* way of knowing it! But then she heard the tall humanoid as he was walking back into the residential section of the cave.

"I decided to see if I could visually scan for the aliens while you were gathering the last of your food," Number 4 said.

But Beeshmah noticed a tiny frown on the mechanical's stylized face. "Did something happen?"

"Actually, young Colonist, it was what *didn't* happen...I know it was a bit of a risk, but I decided to trek back to your camping ground...and everything is intact! Your arboreal vehicle, your tent...it was exactly as we left it days ago!"

The cave was silent as both thought on the matter.

"Why would the aliens ignore—bypass?—my camping site? I don't know about you, 4, but if I were on an alien planet and ran across one of the local's camps, I would want to check it out...or, at least, take something for examination. You and the settlements' elders told us younger ones that is what advanced societies did in history."

Number 4 was nodding, an inquisitive look still on

his face. "And *that* was, indeed, what often happened… from *human* history. Perhaps just as aliens have alien technology and language, maybe their sense of curiosity is also alien to us? Very intriguing. Makes me wonder about all three of the Clans' settlements…if the aliens have the same incurious attitude about *them* as they do for your campsite, perhaps your human sisters and brothers can return to their homes! Assuming they've evacuated them, as I suspect they've done. We can only guess since we don't want to use frequency-tech and be spotted by the aliens."

"Should we load up my land vehicle while we're heading back to the Settlement? Thanks to you, we have enough space in your aircraft now."

That questioning face never left Number 4, as he nodded in affirmation to Beeshmah's question. "Absolutely. As some of you humans say, it looks like we've lucked out!"

She looked at him with squinting, suspicious eyes. "I thought most synthetics don't believe in Luck."

Number 4 began to load some equipment into his aircraft. But he stopped for a second as he looked at Beeshmah. "That's just it; I do *not*…Could be a trap, but yet I am safely *here*, and I do not scan *any* lifeforms anywhere in this region—outside of the ecosystem, of course."

Beeshmah had just finished loading her large wicker bag into the back of Number 4's small aircraft and came back out of the craft, to make sure she had everything of hers from his cave. "What do you think it means?"

Number 4 considered the situation further. "It's rare that I say this, Beeshmah: I simply have no idea."

CHAPTER THIRTY-FOUR

Two of cMaj's moons were out that twilight of the day. The biggest of the trio, Adarah—like the other two, rocky with some ice—dominated cMaj's lightening sky and it shone so bright that it was almost a night-sun! This was because it was the largest moon *and* the closest. Waznii and Tau, the second moon and the smallest of the trio, respectively, were much smaller in the sky. Though, Waznii was the first to dip below cMaj's twilight horizon...all three were named by the humans via the then-Tribal vote many years prior; when the three Clans were still one Tribe of humans.

Back then, the mighty computerable devices, called the *portables*—worn and carried by cMaj's *first* generation of colonists—were a wealth of history and science. They were still in working condition in Miriana's mother's days. They helped provide some of the history of the Canis Major system that the humans, *now*, found themselves in. That single Tribe of humans, then, voted on the names of the three moons, amongst many other subjects that the first generation of colonists had to deal with.

Councilor Mirana Housenn Thuall was still a young woman when she inherited her mother's personal portable.

Miriana remembered how all the portables were able to provide so much help to the humans when it came to learning how to settle cMaj. From geology, agronomy, biology, chemistry, and countless more subjects—plus, there were the *human* scientists from Vestige! Since the portables had expired many years before, and with no synthetic laborers on hand, it was another reason the humans found themselves *back* in the days of ancients, of sorts.

Stranded on cMaj, yet the humans were originally from a high-functioning society...*We are not primitive*, was one of the mantras that all three Clans cited! But, to Councilor Thuall, especially after seeing the attitudes about taking on Number 4 for help with the alien issue at hand, she began to think that the more generations pass from the original Vestige generational starship's colonists, that, perhaps, the vestige of humans *were*, in fact, *devolving*!

Such thoughts were going through Councilor Housenn Thuall's mind as she walked in the nascent daytime, while being cognizant that there was a new humanoid power in that region of the continent. In the back of her mind, Miriana still kept an eye open for the antagonistic, rogue synthetic humanoids. Which made no sense. For it had been years since the height of the human-sythetics skirmishes on cMaj. And now, with the far more advanced aliens, it was anachronistic to worry about such historic conflicts!

It was well over an hour ago that the Councilor had walked out of the cave with her extended family— just after the very frightening experience of hiding in the cave as the aliens passed by with their starship and accompanying army; search-lights beaming and the loud sounds of advanced civilization poured from the very engines of the ship itself!

Yet one more reminder of homo sapiens' lost standing in the universe. For, just 70 years prior, that *used to* be the humans!

She decided to see if she could spot the aliens' convoy in the twilight. Though it had been just over an hour, Miriana figured she might be able to spot their lights at a distance, given the plateau region's flat features in that sector of cMaj's continent...

She took out her photovoltaic binoculars from her bag and surveyed the entire 360-degree horizon of the region...no lights, no aliens.

The Councilor, knowing she was taking a risk, then trekked her way back to the Vestige Clan's settlement! It had been about three weeks since the colonists from all three Clans had evacuated their respective settlements. Well-before she even reached the permanent camp, she could see in the increasing daylight of cMaj that Clan Vestige's settlement was untouched and vacant!

Well, almost vacant...

"*Caradoc*...why in stars are *you* here," Councilor Thuall asked the cMaj Clan leader! She walked over to him briskly and embraced the medium-sized man! They were right on the edge of Vestige Settlement's camp.

A bit younger than her—in his 50s with cropped hair, a long beard, and loose-fitting body wrap, he was a cousin of Miriana from the Sohill side of the family. That is, from her *father's* lineage. On a personal level, the two cousins had *always* gotten along well. From a more

JOSETH MOORE

socio-political point, the cMaj Clan were the first to break from the one-Tribe regime *because* they had agreed with Miriana's mother about the human colonists making peace *with* the rogue synths! The cMaji were allies of the Vestige Clan, in terms of the politics of the rogues. But in tribal *culture*, they couldn't be any further from each other in philosophy!

"I hope you don't mind, Miri...I'm guessing your side of the clandom heard the aliens pass by as well?"

She made a playful, exhausted face; her cousin lightly laughed.

"My clan has been acting more like the Dominions lately, at least when it comes to Number 4..."

They slowly started walking toward the Settlement. Caradoc reacted slightly surprised at his cousin's remark. The Councilor explained.

"Well, you know how it goes: institutional memory of the Synthetic Rebellion! Even when Lanay explains to everyone in *our* generation that Number 4 was the only synth who *helped* us on cMaj during the attack, everyone else just ignores her...and *she's* the one who experienced it; not *them*!"

"They're just scared, Miri. You know the psychology of all that: the arrival of these aliens just brings up deep animosity that's been held in check for several years, since the rogue synths have been less of a threat to humans on cMaj...So, why is Number 4 integral to the alien issue?"

Both were inspecting the grounds and handmade buildings of Clan Vestige's settlement. Both to ensure there were no surprises from the aliens (or the rogue synthetics, for that matter), *and* inspecting for any signs of vandalism from the aliens.

Miriana replied, "You *also* already know this, my friend…just like the three Clans were able to call a kind of truce and try to work together in some kind of way to deal with the visitors, I think we should do the same with 4! Frankly, it's not being neighborly, Caradoc; we *need* Number 4's advanced intellect as a mechanical— especially since humans have lost *all* our portable devices! Plus—"

"—all the synthetics are finally aging, and you want to get as much from all the mechanicals before we lose them all…like we did with the portables."

Caradoc gave an impish look as they both continued their inspection, now walking deeper into the Vestige camping grounds.

Councilor Housenn Thuall gave him a suspicious look before she went down another section of the Settlement. "You've been spying on me!" she called out, knowing it was safe to do so, given she had already checked for the aliens with her binoculars and couldn't see any signs of them.

Caradoc gave a soft chuckle as both, now, silently walked the Vestige Clan's perimeters—ducking into various mastaba-huts, diving under communal structures' outside counters, and cautiously checking every shadow…

After near 15 minutes, the two cousins found themselves on the same rugged pedestrian trail that was linked to a much larger path-system for the entire settlement. There was more of the settlement for them to inspect, but they both came to the same, likely, conclusion.

"So," Caradoc said, after converging on the same trail as the Councilor, "all three Clans have been hiding the caves and bluffs for nothing?"

Councilor Thuall, also, gave a confused look as she surveyed the camp. "This is very odd. Some of us in *our* caves researched some historical references about classic invasions back on Earth and some within Vestige...even with aliens, there are *still* some universal patterns of *how* advanced societies conduct themselves. I'm seeing *none* of that –"

"So far," Caradoc reminded her with one of his index fingers held up. "We can't let our guards down, Miri... this all could be some elaborate trap!"

Councilor Thuall gave her cousin a smirking and appraising look. They both started walking down the trail, farther into Clan Vestige's settlement.

"What amuses you, Cousin," he asked with his own smile while they walked. cMaj's morning was much brighter by that point.

"Recently, Fillah accused me of sounding like a Dominion because I said that if the aliens prove to be nonindigenous, then *we* have every right to claim cMaj as ours...after *your* last statement, Caradoc, it seems that even the spiritually-minded Maji have been a bit affected with the arrival of the aliens!"

The cMaj Clan chief shrugged as they continued their walking inspection of the Settlement. "I take issue of your premise—that *any* group of humanoids thinking they can actually *own* any biosphere or ecosystem is ridiculous, from our philosophy! But that doesn't mean we can't be cautious with those who are enemies to us.

"Funny that we are talking about this, *now*...I was recently reading in one of the history books about a big schism among citizens within the Old Ship, Vestige...It was about 20 years *before* the Synthetics Rebellion! It was a large political movement within Vestige. A group that had a philosophy very similar to that of the Dominionists of today!

"They felt that humans should have split up our population and scatter homo sapiens all over for the explicit purpose of dominating whatever galaxy we found ourselves in—as in, some going toward *this* galaxy, others going to *that* galaxy, while others went...*here*; the Canis Major system!"

Councilor Thuall gave him a questioning look. "Very interesting! I don't think I've ever heard or read about this before. So, whatever happened to these proto-Dominionists?"

A shrug from Caradoc. "Well, there was a relatively small group of citizens that actually ventured out *from* Vestige to try that nonsense of a philosophy! They commandeered a fairly big ship, called the Vasculum Fugae...no one has ever heard from them since! My point is, Cousin, if *we* aren't careful, that could be any of us, today! We should not let our enemies control our emotions so much to the point that *we* react in a rash way!"

"How do we know that the aliens are *enemies*? Did any of the Clans—or the rogue synths, for that matter!—try to reach out and communicate with them?"

It was a concept that the cMaj clan leader had not thought about before! He gave an approving nod.

Before splitting up and searching the rest of Vestige

Clan's settlement, they both stopped walking for a bit. Neither said anything for a while as each looked about the emptied, sprawling permanent camp. Some of the handmade edifices were relatively sophisticated for being constructed with the limited tools available to the Vestigians—mostly crafted of cMaj's cemented soils and rocks with water from nearby ponds and streams. In some cases, wood from the continent's small species of trees were used. Still other buildings were simple mastaba in profile. A few others were built specifically for schools for the Clan's children at various age-levels…

"This is so…irregular," Caradoc finally said, his eyes resting on one of the communal buildings.

"You mean the quiet?"

"And the emptiness of it all…Do you think we should *all* remain in the caves? I've already checked cMaj's settlement. Just like with your village; emptied and no signs of tampering by the aliens!"

Councilor Housenn Thuall took another comprehensive look at the settlement as she sighed. "I would say, yes…you said it yourself: we can't let our guards down! I will say this: given what we've seen how these aliens left our villages untouched, it only reinforces what I've been telling everyone about the acute need for us, humans, to form an alliance with *all* the synthetics!

"Because our visitors are very unpredictable, Caradoc. We already knew they're highly advanced in technology and, therefore, science…" Miriana shook her head while jutting her chin out to indicate the Settlement. "This…all this unpredictable pattern—I'm assuming if they've left our camps alone, they probably did so with the Dominionists' as well. We need the synth's more for their intellect than their physical engineering with the aliens. Especially Number 4—he's got the experience of being a kind of ambassador, *and* his internal actuary programming is biased for it."

Caradoc frowned. "Biased for what, Councilor?"

Miriana thought for a few seconds as they walked. "*Peace...*"

The two finally walked up to the next section of the Vestige Clan's camp. Not much different from the other section they just left. Just a bit more isolated. Construction of a couple of new handmade buildings were underway— interrupted by news of the aliens' arrival.

Caradoc nodded at the Councilor's last statement. They both stopped just before entering the next section of the village.

Caradoc looked upon his cousin with a warning expression. "Well, Cousin, I hope you are right about Number 4. My question is: What if our visitors aren't feeling particularly peaceful?"

CHAPTER THIRTY-FIVE

It was the first time in Beeshmah's life that she had flown, and in this case as a passenger! Her stomach felt queasy whenever synthetic laborer Number 4's homemade aircraft dipped and rose up while the humanoid piloted the rocket-shaped vehicle just a few meters above cMaj's surface! This was to avoid being detected by the aliens. Outside of flying his aircraft, Number 4 kept all other communicative and other electro-tech appliances off, just to make sure *those* could not be captured by the aliens.

They were well-beyond the savanna region at that point and entering the plateaus sector of that portion of the continent, where all the humans resided. This would serve as a good cover for Number 4's craft, as the mountainous plateaus and spires of rock formations blocked a great deal of signals and communications.

As Number 4 and Beeshmah got closer to the wide swath of the platcaus where the three human clans anchored their civilization, Beeshmah could see from the back of the ship, and through 4's dash-console window, various geological structures zoom by—natural archways, columns of rock-edifices, vertical walls of canyon-like plateaus…since Number 4 did not see any utilitarian need to install windows in the back of his aircraft, Beeshmah could only look out of his console; obviously in the anterior of the medium-sized airship. She assumed the synthetic had gotten the window from some vehicle's carcass at starship Vestige crash site, but she didn't want to ask and distract the humanoid while he flew the vehicle.

From the back of the elongated craft, Beeshmah could hear the high-pitched droning sound of the aircraft's ring of metal buzzing around at an incredible 600 revolutions for every minute! This, according to Number 4, before they left his lair, closer to the savanna region. The vertical ring at the center of the rocket-like fuselage of the craft was what had powered the small ship via some nuclear sources that Number 4 tethered to the spinning ring to generate incredible amounts of energy!

Again, Beeshmah had questions about any side effects from those nuclear sources—which, of course, 4 had retrieved from Vestige's crash site. But those curiosities would have to wait until another day...

It took almost another hour before the duo finally reached the general area of the Clandoms. Number 4 took care to park his craft within a ridge that was wide enough for it to fit yet camouflaged by the geological structures surrounding it.

Beeshmah took out her voltaic binoculars from her bag and began to scan the whole area, looking for any signs of the aliens. Number 4 had already done so, but one could not tell just by looking at him—he quietly used his advanced visual actuator systems. Nevertheless, even synthetic humanoids can *still* miss somethings. It was always better to have two sets of eyes on the lookout than one! Plus, in addition to visual inspections, Number 4 scanned the area with various filters and found nothing out of the ordinary.

After making sure that his vehicle was sufficiently hidden and Beeshmah secured her wooden land vehicle at a nearby crevice, Number 4 and the human specialist started to walk toward the general area of the caves and bluffs where all three of the Clans had their temporary encampments. If the two were wrong about the humans escaping to those particular caves, due to the aliens, they could always simply reroute and trek toward the Settlements. No one wanted to risk sending out any frequency comms and be spotted by the aliens, so there was a lot of walking and guesswork involved!

Both were startled when out of nowhere, *four* aircrafts popped up from behind a section of hills, not far from where synthetic Number 4 had landed his skycraft!

The largest of the four belonged to the Dominionists Clan—an irregular-shaped affair with a horizontally protruding fuselage sticking out several yards above the main body of the stubby aircraft. Similar to Number 4's external ring of metal that rotated for nuclear energy, the protrusion of the Dominions' vehicle served as a miniature nuclear fusion chamber. The main body of the aircraft was big enough to seat two passengers plus the pilot, and there was a little room for storage.

One of the other aircrafts, belonging to the Maji, was a cobbled, roundish vehicle just big enough for a pilot and a little storage. On the port and starboard were a bundle of long cylinders that truncated at the ends...both sets of tubes spun furiously and made undulating humming sounds! That was the cMaj Clan's approach to harnessing energy from whatever pieces of debris they retrieved from the mothership's crash site.

The two remaining vehicles were of the Vestige Clan...the two crafts were big enough for only a single-seater and had their two engines on either side of the vehicles. Given they were so small, the Vestigians' aircrafts did not require some oddly-placed attachment for harnessing *their* nuclear source. It was simply stashed away in some compartment of the craft. However, a disadvantage was not having *any* extra room for carrying loads—an extra passenger or badly needed vegetation for food was not an option! The Vestigians' advantage was having *two* aircrafts—being able to have control of cMaj's skies in *two* different places at the same time had its own advantages...

After all four aircrafts landed and their respective hatches opened, members from all three clans exited their vehicles, six, in total—some laughing at the startled reaction of not only Beeshmah, but even the synthetic being next to her! With the exception of the more spiritualistic cMaji colonist among them, *all* were brandishing the most updated weapons that humans could engineer at that time...projectile-shooters: from heavy, dense arrows to menacing rocks, all those sporting a weapon had such projectile-shooters! This was in addition to several classic hand-held weapons—daggers and sharpened stones! All crafted from cMaj's ecosystem, which was one of the advantages of humans living and flourishing on a living planet.

"It worked," Maajida an Preun declared with her

hands raised in the air as she and her cohorts walked out of the largest airship in the gathering. She was the leader of the three-person team from the Dominionists Clan.

By that time, everyone had gathered near Number 4 and Beeshmah. Both had relieved faces after seeing that it was humans and *not* the aliens—or indigenous beings!

"So, 4…how would you rank our cloaking frequency," asked the younger sister of Maajida, Edriel an Preun. She gave a hardy slap on one of the shoulders to their male counterpart in the mission, standing nearby. "Laray's credit! He found the transmission equipment out in the crash site *months* ago!"

The clean-shaven Dominion gave a proud nod. He was a Salomenes—cousin to Beeshmah! But the differences between the Clans was such that they might as well had *not* been related. "Yeah, and I've got the radiation burns to prove it!"

A small round of laughter from the human chauvinists group. The two Vestigians specialists standing nearby and the lone cMaji, all, glanced about uncomfortably. Apparently, they seemed to have shared the same sentiment as Beeshmah and synthetic Number 4 of the Dominionists Clan, in general! But all kept their opinions to themselves.

"We weren't exactly sure how well it worked outside our own testing," Laray explained, a bit more sober at that point. "But, obviously, it does!" He jutted his bald head toward the Maji and the two Vestigians. "Shared the frequency with the other Clans…those aliens maybe superior to us, but we, humans, *still* have the home advantage!"

"If it were a squad of them, we would've had them *all* flaired out by now," Maajida stated forcefully.

"Provided that all there would've been was a small number of them," Ghalen, the Maji, pointed out. cMaj's constant strong winds were whipping around the gathering, causing his long, matted hair and body wrap to flutter. "Don't get me wrong, I give your Clan credit for developing this cloaking frequency, Maajida. I'm simply saying it's a good *defensive* tool against the aliens...plus, we still need to figure out how to keep the signal strong enough for almost 300 colonists!"

Number 4 looked on with fascination of how humans communicated amongst themselves and how they were handling taking on the aliens! It *had* been a while since the humanoid spent much time around homo sapiens!

"So, it seems that you humans have patched things up since I've been away," Number 4 asked. And just as soon as he finished his question, he could already see the shaking of heads by some, including Beeshmah.

"I'm assuming you all held an all-Clan council since I was on my mission, and voted to become allies," Beeshmah asked her fellow humans. "At least, until we get the alien situation figured out..."

"Indeed," Shimon Thuall, one of the two Vestigians, responded. He was one of Councilor Miriana Housenn Thuall's grandchildren. The 20-something continuously looked around the surrounding area, apparently a bit on the paranoid side when it came to the aliens. Tracking signals and photovoltaic binoculars be damned! "Just logic, Beesh...now that the humans have done *our* part, we just need Number 4 to do his and convince the rogues that it's in *their* interest to join in the alliance!"

The young Thuall gave an affirmative nod toward Number 4 with a smile, which was returned with silent nod by the synthetic. The Housenn Thuall families were all good friends with Number 4, since he had always been at the side of their progenitor, Tyra Housenn Sohill.

"It is truly good to see you again, my friend," Shimon stated.

"And you are a young man now, Shimon! In fact, I remember some of you when you were but children… Even we, synthetics, can lose track of how much time goes by!"

Everyone in the knot of humans laughed at Number 4's response!

"Speaking of which," Number 4 continued, "to save time, you won't have to worry about facilitating me…I'm assuming you've all taken to seek refuge in these caves? It was a guess on our part."

"Correct, Number 4," Valda Housenn Salomenes, the other Vestigian in the group, responded.

"Good," he responded with a nod and looked back and forth between Beeshmah and the rest of the humans. "You've completed your mission, Beeshmah. I hope that Shimon and Valda relay to Councilor Housenn Thuall that you've done brave work…I'm not exactly sure where the other synthetics are, but I have been tracking their travel-history over the years.

"I think you make a good point, Shimon, when you say the humans have, at least, formed a loose alliance. When the rogue synthetics hear from me that you've all done this, it makes it more *likely* that the synths will be more willing to join the alliance. Of course, it's not guaranteed, but more likely."

"With the flight-capability they have now, for all we know they could've left this continent," Laray stated, as he, too, glanced about the area, looking out for the aliens.

The five other humans all nodded at Laray's point.

"How will you find them if you can't risk using your scanning abilities and be tracked by the aliens," Ghalen, the oldest of the group, asked. "We don't even know if they're truly alien! Perhaps the continent we're on is just sparsely populated with *their* species...there could be *millions upon millions* of them on the other continents!"

A small chorus from the small group of humans. Even Beeshmah was looking concerned!

"Or," Maajida input, "it could be millions of them on the other side of *this* continent, where we, humans, have not been to yet!"

"That, I can tell you is *not* the case," synthetic Number 4 quickly expressed before the tiny crowd could react to Maajida's comment. Everyone went quiet. "My aircraft is sturdy enough that I was able to traverse this continent a couple of times, *before* we knew about the aliens...in both situations, I absolutely did *not* see any signs of the aliens nor the aliens themselves...from what I saw with my own eyes and scans, cMaj is pretty much the same as the plains regions, the savannas, and the plateau areas here! This continent is pretty consistent, and I saw no signs of any other civilizations, Colonists..."

Number 4's last statement left the humans in deep

thought. All were quietly thinking on the implications before Edriel, one of the Dominions, spoke up.

"Well, that seems to suggest that the visitors *are* aliens!"

More nods from the humans.

"I cannot state that certifiably," Number 4 said, his eyes going to all six humans. "I have not been able to fly to any of the other continents, *yet*. Before Beeshmah went out looking for me, that was the next project I was about to work on..."

There were silent nods from the homo sapiens.

Number 4 could see that Maajida had a thought. He gave a slight nod toward her, indicating that he was listening.

"I think you need *us* to go with you!"

"—What?"

"—We never said anything about that!"

"—I was just thinking about that!"

"Colonists," Number 4 said, his voiced raised a bit to get their attention, as was one of his hands; his face having a slight condescending look to it, "I much appreciate your fervent effort in protecting the Clans—and even me. But I am more than capable of handling this mission on my own...In fact, and I say this without malice, but having others with me would most likely slow me —"

"You mean, like how you *didn't* spot us behind that hill, with our frequency-camouflage," Edriel put to him curtly!

All went quiet, but most of the humans were looking at the synthetic with grins and knowing looks! Indeed, the advanced synthetic humanoid had no reply to the young woman's comment!

"Colonists," Beeshmah came in, partially to help her friend; partially due to more practical concerns, "you realize that with the exception of the aliens and the rogue synths, *every* flying vehicle within cMaj is concentrated right *here*! We all go with Number 4 on this quest, we leave all three Clans *without* an air-defense! Besides, I don't think our vehicles are cobbled together as well as Number 4 did with his craft."

Consent was heard from the other five humans.

"But," Beeshmah came back in, holding up an index finger, "I have to admit, Edriel has a point, 4…not trying to be disrespectful, here, but it's been 70 years since the Synthetic Rebellion that's left you and the other synths marooned here, my friend! *Plus*, you think I didn't notice that you have a little pitting on your epidermal surface from radiation exposure?"

All eyes went to Number 4. Even the mighty synthetic humanoid subconsciously glanced at his aging hands and wrists. Beeshmah went on.

"There was pressure to obtain flight-power after you found out that the rogues started building their own air vehicle almost a year ago. And you beat them to it, 4! I understand. I'm just saying a little help might be in order here…"

Silence, as the laborer synthetic man considered the human's words. cMaj's winds did more than enough to fill the void!

"*If* your chief agrees to it, only the Dominionists Clan's aircraft should go," Number 4 finally said. "I've seen *all* of your aircrafts in action—from a distance in previous times...*theirs* is the most capable *and* has the most spare room, should we need it for an emergency. The three other vehicles *must* stay behind to guard the Settlements...

"Plus..." Number 4 looked at the humans around him. "I'd like for specialist Beeshmah to go with me. She's proven herself on this mission. That is, if you don't mind?"

Beeshmah was beaming! "Not at all, 4! I'll just have to clear it with the Councilor, if you don't mind waiting one more day before heading out? The Dominionists' ship carries *three*...had anyone else in mind?"

Number 4 was already nodding. "And if *you* don't mind, Maajida, since you're already the leader of your team—*and* it's your Clan's ship, and Laray—you showed bravery by going out to the crash site and risk radiation poisoning. Though I highly recommend you never go out there again, for *your* sake. You also figured out how to utilize the frequency-camouflager...there's my mission team.

"Now, I suggest you all go back to your respective Clans. Beeshmah, Maajida, and Laray, let's plan to meet here on the darkest side of the morrow; at the time of Three."

Some from the group of six humans waved their bidding to Number 4 as they trekked their way toward the caves and bluffs. Before they did, a couple of the colonists checked the region with their solar voltaic binoculars for any aliens...aside from the six that were there, plus the synthetic humanoid, there were none to be seen.

CHAPTER THIRTY-SIX

Miriana couldn't help herself from continuously looking over her shoulders, or peer at cMaj's horizon while she was casually walking the perimeters of Lake Thuall…like with most Colonists she had noticed lately, the Councilor was becoming more paranoid about the presence of the aliens! But if it kept one safe and alive from said threat, was it being paranoid?

She had decided to go for one of her long walks, feeling a bit safer; knowing that, for whatever reason, the aliens had no interests in *any* of the Settlements. Of course, as many other Colonists had mentioned amongst themselves in conversations, that simply could be because the *inhabitants* weren't in the Settlement at the time the aliens approached them since all the humans took refuge in some of cMaj's caves and bluffs!

Also, as a precaution, she took along her photovoltaic binoculars and even a smaller version of a projectile-shooter. Both of which the Councilor kept in her small carrying bag, along with her rebuilt comm-device. Like many of the other Colonists, Miriana kept *that* bag tethered to her waist, via a strong, flexible switch from a young tree serving as her belt around her body wrap.

Whenever any of them would venture to the Lake, Miriana and most of the Colonists made sure to maintain several yards *from* the actual shoreline of Lake Thuall because of the sentient sands...that slow, ever-changing beach of living sand organism! The behavior of the sand was very similar to the once-thriving bird populations on the defunct starship of Vestige, especially during flight. Except that the sentient sand glacially moved in sync, and in a group-movement!

The sentientness of the sand was wonderful for photovoltaic technology on cMaj because of their neural connections, but also a source of controversy within the human population on the continent. For it did not sit well with the Maji population that humans were smelting down the sand for purposes of star energy and glass, *and* in doing so with the knowledge that the sand *was* a living organism! It was one of the big issues that the cMaji parted ways from the then-single Tribe system that the humans used to be organized under. That, and, of course, the issue of the humans refusing to agree with working out a peace deal between the humans and the rogue synthetics.

How ironic, Councilor Thuall thought to herself, that the very indigenous, sentient organism on cMaj—at least, in *that* part of the continent—no one cared enough about *it* to the point where humans would *not* utilize the organism. But with the arrival of the visiting aliens, the humans felt threatened by *them*.

More poetry from the Universe...

cMaj's wind was particularly strong that day! The waves from Lake Thuall were lapping against that living shoreline that Miriana was so fond of, and the relatively small clumps of trees arcing parts of the Lake were pushed in the wind's trajectory. The howl of the wind had almost temporarily deafened the elderly woman as she kept walking around the entire lake for the day...

She needed that alone time to think. Think more on what the aliens' next moves could be. Think about if it was a good idea to let young-Beeshmah go on a continental mission on a new flying machine that was not completely proven—and with a couple of Dominions, yet! Think about how to sustainably send out members of her Colony to gather vegetative foods and water while they continued their refuge in the caves, and what latent effects of such living conditions could have on the Clansfolk –

A sudden burst of frequency-interference came from her comm-device!

Councilor Thuall barely caught it, at first, given the high winds that day! She reflexively snatched her small bag from her waist and furiously opened the bag to get her device. Miriana had to cover one of her ears with a freehand so she could hear better while she placed the comm-device to the other ear...

At first, she thought she was having trouble with her device. She pulled it from her listening ear and examined the piece—in working order. But why was she receiving *audio* only? It was an option that was rarely used by most Colonists. In fact, the internal frequency-network that the Clan used—specific to *their* comm-devices, only!—was not a good quality in sound. It was more as a backup, should, for some reason, their higher frequency transmission went down.

She, then, placed the small, cobbled vintage technology

back to her ear. It was *not* a malfunction of her comm nor of the connection…it was then that Councilor Housenn Thuall realized that she was picking up a transmission from the visitors!

CHAPTER THIRTY-SEVEN

Filleppe and Councilor Thuall, both, agreed that she would *not* share her recording that she had made of the transmission from the aliens while out on Lake Thuall earlier that day! To ensure total privacy, and without being outside and risk being tracked by the aliens, they both agreed to quietly venture back to their mastaba-hut so they could play Miriana's recording. They knew that some, within the Vestige Clan, would object to this, since the Councilor had ordered that every colonist from their clan *had* to evacuate the Settlement and find refuge from the aliens either out in the relatively nearby caves or the bluffs…or, as Filleppe rationalized it: it was for an executive reason for breaking her own rule for the rest of the Clan.

She and her common law husband both listened to the recording that Miriana replayed, *several* times! Letting the rest, or even some, within the Vestige Clan know about the transmission would only muddle things for their situation. No doubt in Miriana's and Filleppe's minds, there would be several of their Clansfolk leaving the caves and trying to track down the aliens themselves! And it was definitely outside the thought of sharing it with the two other Clans…

The recording lasted about 20 minutes, before she lost the signal, from when she was at the Lake. The couple were not used to hearing communications that was so static-laden, even by cMaj's standards! But there was no mistaking it, deep within the fluctuating and high-pitched noise, they, both, could hear *voice*! It was impossible to understand, given how faint the voices were and how much frequency disruption had covered those voices. Had synthetic Number 4 been there, he would have been very likely able to record off *her* recording and played it back with enhancements!

A jab of regret for letting Number 4 and specialist Beeshmah go on that mission to find the three rogue synths!

"No other way of boosting this recording," the Councilor asked her husband. They were both seated at the common area's wicker table, hunched over as they listened.

Filleppe gave some thought before responding. "You could zip this to *my* comm, but all I would be able to do is the same thing you can on *your* device, Miri…as the old saying goes: These ain't the Glory Days of Vestige!"

"We need Number 4 to clean this up for us! He *may* even be able to interpret some of what the aliens are saying—based on speech patterns and all that…" Miriana, then, fell back into the backing of the wicker chair that she was seated on, blowing a frustrated sigh.

The recording was played several *more* times… It

was well into the night by the last time they played the recording for the night.

"...the only thing I got is some kind of cadence," Filleppe finally said after a stretch of silence after the last play of the recording. "No surprise...every culture has a cadence when we communicate. Even without Number 4 to help us right now, Miri, did you get *anything* from all this?"

She thought for a while. She was sleepy but determined through the night working with the audio-puzzle with her husband. "At first, it seemed like an open channel—like two different people—beings, talking amongst themselves. But...it could've just been one." Miriana shook her head for lack of understanding.

"Hate to ask after a couple of hours of this, but any chance we simply stumbled across a frequency from the Dominions or the Maji? Maybe even the rogues?"

Again, the Councilor shook her head. "I don't think so...I've ran across some of *their* private frequencies before while on my walks before news of the visitors—and I mean the other Clans *and* the rogues. *None* of them sound like this, Fill! The Clans' are simply signal-blocking where nothing goes through, while the rogue synths' signals are some weird mixture of high and low frequencies—to throw off Number 4, would be my guess."

Filleppe nodded at her observations.

"Let's just sit on this until 4 gets back, Fill."

"Acknowledged," he simply replied. "Just to be safe, did you want to zip it to my comm so we have a backup? Too important to risk losing the recording should something happen to your device."

Without saying a word, Miriana took her comm, dialed some commands on the older interface, and pointed her comm toward his. It took a few seconds, but Filleppe was able to read his comm's monitor and saw that the sharing was successful. He nodded his head upon completion.

"Please be careful with that, Fill...the Clans are already scared. We don't want them to start spreading rumors of an invasion because of a recording they can't understand!"

He looked at his wife and his Councilor with a questioning face. "We've listened to it for two hours and *we* don't understand it...how do we know it's *not* an invasion plan?"

Miriana quietly nodded her head in acknowledging Filleppe's point. "That's why we need to *stay* in the caves and bluffs. And I hope Number 4 and his team are quick with finding *and* convincing the rogues to join our alliance!"

CHAPTER THIRTY-EIGHT

Number 4's and the Dominionists Clan's aircraft had been flying for a week. It was around mid-day in the immediate region that Number 4's team was flying in. The team of three humans and one aging synthetic humanoid stopped only for the humans to refresh themselves, and even that was just a few times. It was not lost on the humans that Number 4 was actually right when he said that having others go with him (i.e., *humans*) would only slow him down. Otherwise, the humans took shifts in flying the Dominionists' craft while the other two slept, ate, or simply rest. That way, the airship could continue flying virtually nonstop. And when the two-vehicle team *did* stop for a short while, they all made sure to scan for any signs of the aliens along with looking for their targeted objective, the rogue synthetics.

As the team got further to the east on the continent, and several hundreds of miles from the starship Vestige crash site and the human Settlements not too far from *it*, cMaj's landscape change a fair amount—the arid lands transformed to verdant flatlands with scores of small lakes and ponds dotting various sections of the region. There were some moderate mountains as well, but not quite as large as the plateaus of the humans' home-region. Otherwise, as Number 4 told the small knot of humans a week prior, cMaj's ecosystem was mostly consistent.

The team made sure not to communicate via their frequencies on their comm devices. Again, in order to avoid attracting the attention of the visitors. Number 4 had communicated with the three humans when the team had done their rest-stops for the Colonists. Whatever else the humans needed or wanted to tell the synthetic would have to wait until their next rest-stop.

The team flew their two hodgepodged vehicles at low altitudes—avoiding detection from the aliens. The use of the camouflaging frequency emitter worked better for things and people when they were not in motion. But, as with any other signals, if said items were mobile *and* using the frequency-camouflager, detection was still more of a possibility. So, though both aircrafts were using the camouflager, they still had to exercise precaution.

The team still was not sure how much presence the alien species was on the continent, even this far into the mission while looking for the rogue synths. As Number 4 told the young humans, he had *not* seen anything to indicate any advanced civilizations dwelling on the continent.

But Ghalen, the cMaji of the small group from the week prior, made a good point: it was *possible* that the continent they were on was simply a lightly populated portion of the planet of cMaj. The two times Number 4 had traversed the continent did not necessarily mean an alien society was not there. Though, logic seemed to suggest Number 4 was right.

The humans *were* right about one major point: Number 4 did *not* anticipate their frequency-camouflager. So, what about a far more advanced alien species' capability? It was certainly possible that the visitors could have been using their *own* camouflaging transmission and the team not know it!

Beeshmah, however, made a very poignant observation during one of the team's break from flying and they all converged for an impromptu meeting: earlier in her hunt for Number 4—when the synthetic had rescued her from the encroaching aliens at that time—they did not bother using *any* kind of blocking or camouflaging technology *then*. So, as one followed the logic, why would the aliens decide to use such transmission *now* just because they were on the other side of the continent?

Also, would not an alien force, upon arriving on a new planet, be more cautious about *their* approach to said planet? This was Number 4's observation...Laray's response was, also, very poignant: the visiting aliens' *behavior* almost seemed as if they felt at home and did not have to worry about whether or not any other species had seen them! This was, yet, one more point that seemed to indicate that the so-called aliens might have been indigenous after all!

Just as Councilor Housenn Thuall said to the cMaj leader, many days previously and separately from Number 4's team, the aliens were, indeed, very unpredictable! And, hence, more dangerous...

On one of the droning days of flight, both aircrafts picked up two signals approximately two miles ahead of the team! The detecting technology used aboard both aircraft were from separate, defunct machines from the Vestige crash site but very much in working order!

Without using their comms, Number 4 and Beeshmah—as it happened to be her shift to fly—automatically halted their respective vehicles and quickly maneuvered them behind the closest clump of trees they could find in the semi-mountainous region!

The two aircraft were several yards from each other's hiding place. Number 4 and Beeshmah quickly turned off every system within their own vehicle, to ensure no risk of detection. The only exception was the aircraft's frequency-camouflager! At that point, it was all about visually detecting whatever the two blips were! Beeshmah, Maajida, and Laray all went into a nervous silent mode in the eerie quiet of the Dominionists aircraft...even out in the eastern portion of the continent cMaj's winds howled and shook the parked aircrafts within the small gathering of trees!

It was times like these that it was actually a *disadvantage* in being a synthetic being. For Number 4's cybernetic genetics and actuator systems could also be detected, depending on how detailed another being's scanning was! The humans, inherently, did not have this problem, given their biological makeup. The only protection Number 4 had at that time was his vehicle's shielding from the camouflage emitter!

The Dominionists vehicle creaked under the buffering of the winds. That creaking, the trees' limbs scratching against the exterior of the aircraft, and the wind were the only things making any sound...except for the nervous breathing of the humans! They couldn't even tell how big the two targets were, given the somewhat primitive detection system they were using before Beeshmah had to quickly turn everything off.

Two miles was a short distance for any flying machine, so Number 4 and the humans knew it would be just seconds before the two entities would pass them. Perhaps 100 yards or so. But, again, when dealing with the speed of flying vehicles, yards would take only *seconds* to traverse!

Number 4 would have usually used his visual-enhancers to get a closer look at a distant object. But those, too, posed a risk of detection. So, he had to look with his synthetic eyes the same way that that humans had to...it was a very rare occasion when Number 4 felt so vulnerable! He pitied humans, at that quiet moment, for all their inherent vulnerabilities.

Then, about one minute later, two figures flashed over the immediate horizon, the direction where Number 4's team was heading! The objects blurred by and went westward...the phenomenon was a bit too quick for the humans, but not for Number 4!

Without warning, the humans were able to see through the Dominionists vehicle's cockpit that Number 4 had re-engaged his spinning metallic ring and his aircraft swiftly shot up from his grouping of trees and the craft bolted in the same direction as the two targets!

"What in stars is he doing," Maajida bit out as she threw herself back into her seat and buckled into it!

"Comm him," Laray insisted from his own seat as he, too, snapped on his restrainer.

"Aliens, Laray," Beeshmah reminded him as she began to revive their ship! "Besides…it's *them*!"

The two Dominions thought hard for a bit while Beeshmah maneuvered the odd-looking airship from their hiding place and quickly advanced the ship to follow Number 4's craft! Not surprisingly, none of the humans' airships were cobbled together as well as Number 4's. So, the humans took a little while before they began to catch up with Number 4's vehicle.

"You mean the rogues," Maajida asked as she craned, trying see beyond their cockpit.

"Why are there only *two*," Laray noted as he looked on nervously.

Beeshmah was already shaking her head, keeping her eyes on the situation ahead of them. "I don't know…hope nothing happened to whichever is missing. We need all *three* for our alliance against the aliens to work!"

"*If* they even agree to work with us," Maajida pointed out.

Laray subconsciously nodded in response. Beeshmah did not bother to reply…

Laborer synthetic Number 4 was able to surpass the two jetting synthetic humanoids with his airship— shooting above them while actually increasing his speed so he would have enough time to turn his vehicle around and cut them off, should they decide to split up and make it harder for *their* predators to hunt them…for, the rogues were not in official contact with the humans nor Number 4, so it was not known within the team if the rogue synths knew about the airships built by the three Clans and Number 4.

Knowing this, plus keeping in mind about not using his comm to avoid detection from the aliens, Number 4 quickly flashed his craft's forward lights in a code that was, more or less, universally understood as, *I come in peace.*

It worked! The two artificial humanoids immediately slowed down before they came to a complete halt, hovering above cMaj's ground before finally landing on their feet. Their built-in rockets, designed just like Number 4's, quickly disengaged and disconnected as single units and furled into each rogue synth's upper-back; between the shoulder blades.

All four synthetics on cMaj made a point to fabricate their body wraps so that a slit ran vertically on the upper-back side, to accommodate their small portable rockets. The rogues had adapted many years ago to wearing their body wraps to be closer-fitting—much easier to fly around in via their jet units, than the more loose-fitting wraps that *humans* wore on cMaj.

Beeshmah had landed the Dominionists airship nearby. After a truncated discussion, all three humans decided to stay inside the vehicle, to give a bit of space for the synthetics to talk amongst themselves. It had been, perhaps, several *years* since Number 4 had talked with any of the other three synths.

In *that*, the synthetic humanoids were similar with humans, from a psychological viewpoint. What was *not* similar was what the three humans observed as they watched the trio of synths: The two rogues were standing closer to each other and Number 4 was slightly distant from them…they formed a silent, tiny statuary. *None* of them verbalizing any of their conversation!

Beeshmah, Maajida, and Laray thought that the synthetics had suffered some technical problems! But then all three remembered that, as artificial beings, the synths did not *need* to *talk*. They did that while in the presence of humans, *for* the humans, so they could communicate with the synths. And, so long as they stood close to each other, their internal signals only went out a few inches and could not be tracked by the aliens.

Beeshmah didn't care *how* Number 4 conferenced with the rogues. She just hoped that the very last synthetic laborers that had helped conspire to destroy the Mothership, Vestige, just over 70 years ago, could be trusted in a coalition against a new and far more advanced enemy. If, indeed, the aliens proved to be such.

In the meantime, the *other* trio—the humans— decided to take advantage of the time and relaxed or slept in their seats within the Dominionists aircraft.

CHAPTER THIRTY-NINE

It had been about two weeks since Vestige Clan members Valda Housenn Salomenes and Shimon Thuall had seen synthetic Number 4, when they and a few other humans were on the watch for the aliens. Since then, they had been conducting their duty as sentries.

The two Vestigians were given a good amount of autonomy for how they decided to conduct their surveillance, per Councilor Miriana Housenn Thuall. They divided the cave-system and bluffs that the Vestige Clan had occupied into different sections between them, since they were the two clan members that fabricated the ships—along with Miriana's son, Fillamon. And because of that, Valda and Shimon mostly flew the two aircrafts that belonged to the Clan. It was only until the Councilor had found out about the two small ships did the practice of guard duty become a part of the Clan's more aggressive posture toward the alien issue. As cMaj politics went, it was not quite aggressive enough for a faction within the Vestige Clan; Fuegon Sohill an Preun being the leader of that corner of the Clan.

Since all three clans had agreed to form a temporary alliance to tackle the alien issue, part of the agreement was that since Number 4 was using the Dominionists Clan's airship on his mission, the Vestigians had to divvy their air-time with their two crafts with *them*. Hence, Shimon and Valda would spend alternating days over in the Dominionists' section, patrolling while the other guarded Vestige's turf.

Shimon and Valda also taught a few of the Dominions how to fly *their* airships. Rhett, chief of the Dominionists Clan, insisted that his people have free access to the Vestigian ships as part of the deal. Councilor Thuall felt it was going too far, but she made the agreement with the Dominions for the sake of keeping the fragile alliance intact!

Since the Maji had their own, though small, aircraft, they did not need to make such agreement with the Vestigians.

That particular night, it was Shimon, one of Miriana's grandchildren, who was scheduled to do guard duties at the Dominionists' refuge site. On a personal aspect, he did not care for the clan! Nor did the majority of the clan members from Vestige and cMaj. But, since Shimon was a *Thuall*, it was a bit more personal since his grandmother was talked about quite rudely by Dominions, given the Vestige Clan was seen as a rival to the Dominionists. Indeed, everyone noticed that the Dominions may have not shared anything with the Maji, but they did not excoriate them like they did the Vestigians. And Miriana Housenn Thuall, especially.

Since the humans had developed the photovoltaic binoculars with the smelting of sentient sand and polishing the resulting glass so that it had visually magnifying properties, they were able to monitor event and locales when there weren't enough leftover detectors from the Vestige crash site. One of the features that Shimon *wished* they had was spectral observation. That is, being able to see the landscape at night! His generation had heard from the elders that the population within the Old Ship was able to do this, amongst a great deal of other highly advanced abilities! All three moons were out, but the light reflected from them onto the surface of cMaj just was not enough for the humans to peer into the shadows of nighttime...

As he took sweeping looks of the region in the night with his binoculars, Shimon thought on such things. Indeed, there were some among the younger generations from all three Clans that wondered if their ancestors on the historic Vestige starship were just as advanced as the aliens were!

It felt so backwards to Shimon. Indeed, to all the youngest of the humans: that the *ancestors* of homo sapiens, even during deep history, were *far* more technologically advanced than the contemporary society they found themselves in! Even Shimon and his generation knew that, generally speaking, throughout the history of humanity, humans were on a progressive arc of development—not just with technology, but of the human mindset and civilization.

That unfortunate word that his generation had inherited from the elders, *Singularity*, was responsible for the situation they *all* found themselves in at that moment. There was a pang of regret from the young Thuall that *his* generation of humans could have been at a much more powerful stance against the aliens, had not the Synthetic Rebellion occurred...

Shimon, Valda, and the Dominions that they had trained to fly the two Vestige airships, learned to fly the vehicles at very low altitudes and even to park the crafts quickly within crevices of the plateaus—should the aliens unexpectedly pop up within the region. It was just a few weeks ago when this happened, so the Clandoms wanted to make sure they were not caught off guard so badly as all three clans were that night!

But that particular night, it was quiet...a night of stasis, as much was possible on cMaj. The winds of cMaj were about the only major event that was occurring! And that was how Shimon preferred it.

After taking another walkabout in the Dominionists refuge area, he went back to where he hid the parked Vestigian aircraft he was flying and sat on an outcrop close to the vehicle; a good place with back support so Shimon could relax. He had trained himself to sleep on alternating cycles, for his sentry duties. Nevertheless, the young Thuall drifted asleep under cMaj's dark skies.

CHAPTER FORTY

"Why is everyone gathering here...is there something wrong," Councilor Thuall asked the group of young Vestigians.

She was coming back to the cave system that the Housenn Thuall extended families refuged in from the aliens. It was her turn, along with a few other family members, to gather vegetation for the families. Miriana and Filleppe made it a point that they, also, participated in the gatherings just like any other family members. From what she heard from one of her several specialists that spied and did various odd jobs for the Councilor, Chief Rhett of the Dominionists Clan left such mundane tasks to others in *his* clandom.

All the young ones, gathered at the mouth of the cave, turned to look at the Councilor as she approached and talked over one another excitedly! One of them, Paul Salomenes Thuall, held up a comm device that belonged to one of the adults.

"Thanks to Gurna's father, we finally have moving pictions of them, Councilor," the teenager whispered harshly! It was his way of being mindful of keeping his voice down in case the aliens were nearby…indeed, apparently, not so far off!

Miriana froze!

"You—you have what?"

"Animated pictions, Councilor," came Gurna an Preun's impatient voice. She was part of the extended family by means of a new pairing of the an Preun and Housenn families. "My father spotted them when he was out for the gathering earlier today! He didn't go to the Settlement, Councilor—honestly! He just used his magnifier and recorded what he saw…please don't be mad with him!"

She quickly sat her basket of vegetation and roots down and ran over to where the adolescents were. She gave Gurna a hurried hug to let her understand that she was not crossed with her father. She snatched the device from Paul's hand, though the device belonged to Gurna's father. He was holding it out for her. The vid was playing in a loop, so all the Councilor had to do was look upon the scratched-up monitor within the antique device.

"This was taken from our Settlement," Miriana said aloud. More to herself than to the young Vestigians surrounding her. She watched with a mixture of anticipation, horror, and puzzlement…

It was a relatively clear piction of the Vestigian permanent campsite from a distance. It was a bit on the shaky side, and one could hear Nascent Housenn an Preun, Gurna's father, breathing nervously behind the footage! And walking with an awkward gait, several beings were seen on the piction; treading all over the Settlement!

All were of the same profile: Four-legged but with a torso similar to a human being's, but their stance was such that their torso was horizontal—giving the look as if a human being had both feet *and* both pairs of hands on the ground and lifted up their buttocks! And where a human head would have been, there was, in fact, an irregular protrusion sticking up—as if the head were at the back of the body, looking straight out from the chest area as they walked!

In the moving piction, which sometimes went out of focus while Nascent recorded the footage, Councilor Thuall could tell they were not wearing clothes as such. But it looked as if they had some kind of body-fitted apparel.

The beings moved smoothly, despite their unusual leg-motion. Some went into some of the vacant handmade buildings of the Settlement while some of the other beings walked the perimeter of the township or down the pedestrian network that connected the Settlement!

"Where is your father now," Councilor Housenn Thuall put to the young woman as she handed the comm device to her.

"They're in the back of the cave, Councilor...they were having an emergency meeting until you got back!"

"Inside...all of you," Miriana whispered in a more hushed tone that time. "Now! Come on..."

She knew that her common law husband had already made it back to the cave. But Miriana always made sure she was the last to return to the cave system when she went out with others.

There was pandemonium among the extended

families! They had the mind to whisper, but as Miriana made her way back to the deeper portion of the cave she could see absolute fear and even excitement within her family's countenances, due to Nascent's recording!

The back portion of the cave was a location the Housenn Thuall families utilized for business meetings that needed to be private from the rest of the Housenn Thuall house. When Miriana made it back there, she found six members scrunched over someone's comm device as they analyzed the recording with the aliens crawling all over Settlement Vestige!

Her common law husband, Filleppe, and their son, Fillamon, were there. As was one of the Councilor's specialists, Fuegon. The others were Shamira Thuall, Lieu Natsome Housenn, and Nascent, the one who recorded the piction of the aliens at the camp…Shamira was a middle-aged 'singleton,' as humans called people who did not have their own family. While Lieu, also of mature age, was a family member from Filleppe's side—from *his* father, Fillip Natsome.

"Councilor," came the chorus from all six as Miriana arrived at the small meeting; even her husband, especially whenever business was being conducted within the Clan.

"I played the audio that you recorded of them from the Lake," Filleppe informed Councilor Thuall. He wasn't sure if she would be happy about that, given they had been keeping that information away from the rest of the entire Clan. But Miriana merely nodded her head. After seeing that, Filleppe continued with a tiny bit of relief. "We just started examining the vid from Nascent…it's not really *them*, Councilor."

At that point, Miriana froze for confusion. "Last time I've seen humans, Filleppe, we didn't look anything like *that*! So, if it's not the aliens, who *are* they?"

Shamira, wearing handed-crafted spectacles derived from the sentient sands—though not fitted perfectly to her face, signaled to the others that she would respond to Miriana. "Councilor...what did our ancestors used to do on starship Vestige when they would run across a planet, moon, or asteroid that needed to be examined *or* explored?"

"Well, besides the use of scanning technology they had back then, they would send probes," Councilor Thuall said with an impatient shrug as her eyes glanced at everyone in attendance.

"Exactly...you all know that I'm somewhat of an historian. I've studied the books on history that *your* mother oversaw their production by synthetic Number 4 and all the old portables we had at the time. Plus, about as many projected vids. Our ancestors crafted various types of probes that reflected *our* human form, *most* of the time."

"You're talking anthropomorphism," Fuegon pointed out with a single, terse nod.

"Exactly," Shamira confirmed. "Besides, take a close look at them...they're *too* uniform. Much like how our ancestors used to design the synthetics!"

"So," Councilor Thuall stated, catching on to what Shamira was saying, "these—creatures...these beings are some kind of vanguard of the aliens and gives us a clue how *they* might look like?"

"Exactly! Just like the synthetics."

"But not *all* mechanicals that we, humans, used to

make reflected us," Lieu pointed out. "No more than our old actuator vehicles or the different types of synthetic laborers that were on Vestige. I *still* say, for all we know, the aliens could look like the Tardigrades-slugs!"

There were smirks at Lieu's quip! The small group continued to look at the looped vid on the device.

"Well, regardless of what these...quadrawalkers are, they're a bit too close to the caves and bluffs for my comfort," Nascent said as he glanced toward the front area of the long cave, seeing how all the extended family members were doing.

Nods and voiced consent were heard in the small circle.

"I wonder if they're also ransacking the Dominionists and the Maji," Fillamon input.

That got Miriana thinking. She cupped her chin with one of her hands. "Focus on how *fast* they were moving about in our village..."

After a few seconds of silent observations from the group, Filleppe finally spoke up. "They're *not* ransacking, are they? I don't see any containers with them to indicate that they are stashing away stollen items—"

"—or carrying anything *with* them," Shamira pointed out.

"Could they be dispersing some kind of poison," Fuegon asked.

All went quiet to think on the young Sohill an Preun's question.

"That's possible," Fillamon interjected. "*If* they are what you suggested, Shamira, they might be some mix of mechanical *and* biological beings and store some chemicals within them! But…" He took a few seconds to stoop down to get a closer look at the moving piction of the quadrawalkers in the Vestige settlement on the device. "Too hard to tell from this vid. But, Fuegon, you bring up something we definitely should be cautious of whenever we move back into the settlement."

Some in the group looked at Fillamon with surprise! Lieu spoke what was on the others' minds. "Fillah, what do you think is happening, here? We have *no* idea how long the aliens are going to be here. This, my friend, is officially an invasion now!"

"Hate to say it, my son," Filleppe came in, "but these living arrangements the Clans find ourselves in could be permanent!"

Just hearing Filleppe say his last statement was enough to shut down the small gathering for nearly a solid minute…

"You're right, Lieu," the Councilor of the Clan finally spoke up, after deliberately holding back to let others have their say, "this is, *now*, an invasion!" Miriana then turned and said while looking at the bespectacled historian, Shamira, "Traditionally speaking, in the days of ancient, it would automatically be a state of *war* between the two societies…"

"But we are in no position to fight against *three* aging rogue synthetics, Councilor," Fuegon, now, said; tinged with irritation! "I hope you are not suggesting that this weak human alliance will have some kind of chance of winning a war with these advanced aliens?"

Nascent was shaking his head, agreeing with Fuegon. "We've all seen the piction that Chief Rhett has of their huge ship with several hundreds of *them* under it! Sheer numbers, alone, we'd lose—to say nothing of their technology!"

Fillamon was looking at his mother, waiting to see her response. But she let him say what was on *his* mind. "Councilor, I know you have faith in Number 4, and not just because he was a loyal friend of your mother. But even if we're able to get all three rogues *and* Number 4 with us in this alliance…"

Fillamon slowly shook his head while keeping his eyes on the looping vid. He, then continued.

"I understand that all synths have an ability with lancing flames, flight, speed, and their advanced artificial thinking, but I'm certain it would be a war that *all* of humanity would lose! I don't need to remind anyone that there's only a few of us left in all the universe…"

Fillamon looked around the group of seven. It was a softly spoken warning about any ambitious plans against the aliens!

By that time, Miriana glanced at her husband. "And what of the audio recording I did from Lake Thuall…that was *them*, correct?"

Filleppe was nodding but let the younger Vestigians answer for him. Nascent spoke up.

"We only had a chance to listen to it once before your arrival, Councilor. But from what your husband showed us, your signal was on a different frequency than what I used for my recording of these quadrawalkers…I can't say I got much in the way of audio, but what audio I *did* record *with* my visuals, it's clear that these walkers' signals for communications are completely different from what I heard from yours."

Lieu also came in. "Put simply, Councilor Thuall: *you* recorded the actual aliens on audio; Nascent, here, visually recorded *their* version of synthetic beings."

"And we still couldn't discern anything from all the interference," Fuegon contributed. "Just like you and Filleppe...I'm sure Number 4 or any of his synth brethren could!"

"So," asked Shamira, "what do we do now, Councilor? It seems as though the aliens are inching closer to our refuge spot and from what I know, we don't have a secondary backup!"

There was complete silence within the small group. The chatter from the front of the cave among the house of the families of Housenn and Thuall were non-stop as they, too, were trying to figure things out with the visitors.

"The crash site," Filleppe simply stated. All eyes cut to him. "That's the only secondary backup I can think of...I know it's a couple of hundred miles from here and won't do us any –"

"That's ingenious, father!" Fillamon said excitedly as he and Shamira and Fuegon all exchanged a shared epiphany! Fillamon continued. "Yes, it's much too far for the entire Clan to evacuate to—"

"—but it would make a great *diversion* from the rest of *us* if we take one or two aircrafts and fly them to the site," Shamira added.

Miriana, Filleppe, Lieu, and Nascent all glanced at each other, not receiving the vision that the others saw!

"Ok," Councilor Housenn Thuall said, trying to play along. "And once said-colonists arrive at the crash site, they...Stars! That's where we can use the synths!"

"They're not as badly affected by the nuclear radiation like humans," Fuegon said, beaming while nodding his head.

"They have their installed jets," Nascent reminded the circle. "Will they even *need* a ship? Couldn't they simply fly out there? That way we can use all six airships between the humans and the synthetics!"

There were a couple of skeptical faces at that point.

"Their jets are for low-flight," Filleppe responded. "More of augmentation than long-term transportation. Still, you make a good point, Nascent. I just hate to see them left with only their jets for transportation, should things take a turn for the worst out there with the aliens! So, what would *they* do, while out at the crash site to keep the aliens away?"

Councilor Thuall, again, in keeping with her approach to leadership, refrained from saying anything to let her impromptu circle of counsel work things out. A couple of the colonists shrugged, but Fuegon ventured a response.

"I say we keep the plan simple—they're synthetic humanoids, they'll be able to strategize things out for themselves without us needing to plot for them! But I would guess since we're talking about a big *city* that crash landed out there, the synths would have ample space and hiding locations."

Shamira shifted uncomfortably as she adjusted her spectacles. "Just don't like the idea of the synths simply *hiding* from the aliens to keep them busy while we, humans, *still* wouldn't be able to do anything against the aliens—defensive-wise! I understand your point, Fuegon, about letting the synths devising their own plans while out there, but is there something we can have them *do* while out there that would further the protection of *all* the populations of cMaj? It *is* an alliance that we've formed with the other Clans and the rogues, after all! What's the point if we don't think in holistic terms?"

Couple of others nodded in agreement with Shamira; a couple of others had skeptical faces.

"Actually, I was just thinking while you made your point about having the synths do something on behalf of the humans *and* all four synths..." Filleppe subconsciously glanced at the looping vid on the device that was propped on the outcropping the circle of colonists was using at that time. "We *still* haven't heard from Number 4's team yet! I know we can't risk comm'ing them to see how their mission went, but we're operating with the assumption that the rogues would even *agree* to our alliance!"

That time, all six of the others in the meeting were nodding their heads. A couple of them reacted as if they had forgotten about such an important point!

"Well," Lieu said with arched brow and a sigh, "I can't say I would blame them. After we, humans, turned *their* peace gesture down all those years ago!"

There were begrudging shrugs and nods at Lieu's observation.

"Granted, Filleppe," the Councilor stated, coming back into the discussion. Miriana's eyes shifted to the entire circle. "So, let's say the rogues did *not* agree to join our alliance? What's our backup, when it would be just us, humans, and only one synthetic with us?"

That time, the responses from the tiny committee was silent for a long while. Shaking of heads, shrugs, and wondering eyes were what was communicated at that time!

"Hate thinking this would be the case," Fillamon said, breaking the long silence, "but we'd probably keep with the same plan. Just with *one* synthetic—Number 4!"

"Have him fly out there," Lieu input, "and create some kind of diversion...hopefully, where he doesn't put himself at too much risk with either the aliens *or* the radiation!"

"Ok," Nascent, was pointing out, "seems like we have no choice in *that* part of the plan—the crash site it *is*, if I may say so, Councilor?" Miriana simply nodded and let him continue. "Now, what about on *our* end, as you alluded to, Shamira? What can *we* humans do against the aliens while—worst case scenario, and it's *only* Number 4 joining the alliance, *and* he's out at the crash site drawing attention away from us? Should we even *try* defensive strategies since we, humans would be out in the caves and bluffs by ourselves? It seems we've *already* decided earlier that they are *too* advanced for us to even *try* to fight them! Maybe we're simply outmatched and should—"

"—Move," Fuegon interjected. His mere question was effective at pointing out the flaw of Nascent's speculation.

A pocket of silence after that exchange.

"Good point," Filleppe came in. "And it wouldn't be just *our* clan. Where would almost 300 people evacuate to when we've already found refuge in the caves and bluffs?

The aliens *are* inching their way *here*! Again, as you said, Nascent, taking the worst-case scenario, it would only be Number 4 *plus* five air machines to use—*small* ones, at that! Wouldn't do any good for the majority of the entire human population…"

Fuegon glanced at everyone, gauging their attitudes. "So…we can't just *hope* the aliens don't find us while they play a game of the seeker and the hidden with any of the synths out at the crash site!"

There was that uncomfortable silence in the small circle of colonists again. At that moment, Councilor Housenn Thuall spoke up again.

"Unfortunately, it seems that's what we're finding ourselves having to do, Fuegon…"

CHAPTER FORTY-ONE

"**B**e careful, Laray," Beeshmah admonished the Dominion, as he peeped his head over the looming outcrop! "Just because we're using our camouflager, it doesn't mean we're *totally* invisible!"

He was looking through his photovoltaic binoculars and trained them on the cMaj Clan's settlement…Number 4's team had made it back about a day previously with a precious gift: two of the three rogue synths! The team of three humans and now *three* synthetic humanoids were surprised to find the Maji's tiny village overran by some sort of creepy alien forms crawling about the camp!

"Stars, and I thought the Tardigrades were bad," Maajida commented softly as she, too, looked on with her binoculars.

The whole team of six was clumped together, behind a jungle of rock formations that was not far from Clan cMaj's bluffs refuge.

"Well, now we're *really* at war with them," Laray said as he slid down from his perch and stashed his looking device into his portable bag. "I can't imagine the aliens occupying only *one* human camp!"

"It was a wise judgement of you humans to vacate all

of your settlements, indeed," commented Ascent, one of the rogue synthetic humanoids.

His body wrap, as was his present *rogue* companion, Forward On, was different from Number 4's. It reminded the three humans in the team of the historical pictions of *their* ancestors...*pants* and *shirts*, was how such articles of clothing were called.

Apparently, the synthetics had more time on their hands to farm cMaj's vegetation and utilized the husk from said greenery and fashioned such vestments. Beeshmah understood that their clothing made it easier for them to fly around with their jets, but from her perspective it showed, yet, one more layer of difference the synthetics had from the humans.

"Colonists," Forward On said as he continued to look from his hiding spot, using his magnifying features of his eyes, "you realize that those are very similar to *us*..."

Beeshmah, Maajida, and Laray all whipped their heads around to look at Forward On. *All* had a curious expression!

Number 4 had a smirk on his face. "It's just a guess, humans, but those crawlers appear to be a cybernetic being of some sort..." Number 4 jutted his chin toward the settlement, much like a human would. "Without being able to use our scanning features for the moment, I can tell by their gait and almost copied profiles."

"It was one of the reasons *why* we chose names for ourselves," Ascent said. "So you, humans, would be able to distinguish us a bit more. No, colonists, those things are the servants of our visiting friends!"

"Hmm," Maajida expressed, the tone of offense to it!

There was an uneasy quiet amongst the team.

"Did I say something wrong," Ascent asked, breaking the uneasy silence.

"Ascent," Number 4 said with some impatience, "when we first talked on the other side of the continent, I told you both that quite a few of the humans have not...*forgotten* what all three of you took part in during the Synthetics' Rebellion! When you say, *servant* under these circumstances—those synthetics working for an unseen biological *master*, it comes across as distastefully inappropriate when it is *from* a synthetic...much less *from* one that was one of the offending insurrectionists."

Ascent and Forward On looked at all the humans and then at each other. Then re-directed their attention on Number 4. The humans all watched, keeping their comments to themselves, for the time being.

"I'm assuming you mean some *collective memory* when you say this," Forward On commented.

"As *I* understand it," Ascent came back in, "you told us there was only *one* original survivor of the explosion—"

"—bombing!" Laray and Maajida said simultaneously!

Beeshmah and Number 4 both indicated that they *all* needed to be quiet with the crawlers down the way at the Maji Settlement!

Ascent resumed, whispering. "*None* of the other humans, besides that former pilot, were even born yet, and by *several* decades! This is too poetic to say that humans have some supernatural, shared memory. As synthetics, Number 4, *we* don't even have that!"

"Ascent," Forward On interjected after taking another quick look toward the cMaj camp with the alien beings amongst it, "perhaps it is best we not discus this… especially with the planet's newest power occupying the humans' homes not very far from us?"

There was silence amongst the team. They all resumed watching the walkers with their binoculars.

"You, synths never got a chance to tell us *where* Majoreen is," Beeshmah whispered, her binoculars still up to her eyes.

"He's returning from one of the other continents closest to *this* one," Forward On informed with a whisper, as he, too, kept his eyes on the camp. "Just after we spotted the aliens several weeks ago, we all agreed that one of us should see if it were viable to try to re-locate to another continent with the arrival of these visitors."

All the humans were nodding at Forward On's revelation.

"Wish we could do that," Laray softly admitted.

"Hey…they're leaving," Beeshmah said with a surprised and hushed voice!

"Should we follow them," Maajida asked any of the synthetics.

"Or maybe *one* of you," Beeshmah suggested. "That way we can, at least, have an idea *where* they are!" She shrugged.

"I think since I have a trusting relationship with most of the humans, I should go," Number 4 said after, apparently, the three synthetics had discussed the situation between themselves via their intra-network, safely from the aliens. Basically, it was equivalent to the original Vestige colony's cerebral-comm for humans. The communication technology eventually lost their powers among the *first* surviving humans many decades previously.

Of course, Number 4's suggestion meant that the three humans would have to go to their respective clans and informed them that two of the surviving rogue synths from the Bombing—which *they* participated in—had arrived at *their* refuge site; ready to join the shaky alliance against the formidable aliens!

But Ascent insisted that the two synthetic laborers would find their own cave, near the humans' hiding zones. That way, when they needed the artificial humanoids, they weren't that far away.

The three humans and Number 4 agreed. The team watched and waited a few more minutes while the oddly marching beings split up into smaller groups and went in different directions, leaving the cMaj Clan's small village. From what the team could see at that moment, none of the alien synthetics were heading in *their* direction.

Number 4 suggested that the others of the team wait inside their air vehicles—the humans to the Dominionists Clan's airship while the two rogue synths could wait in Number 4's ship. He had made room for a second person to fit after he had swooped up Beeshmah and took her to his cave out in the savanna region, while escaping the aliens. This was just in case the rest of the team needed to quickly take to cMaj's skies, should the crawlers surprise them while Number 4 spied on the alien synthetics.

CHAPTER FORTY-TWO

Councilor Housenn Thuall welcomed specialist Beeshmah Salomenes back to the clandom with a toned-down official recognition amongst the entire Vestige Clan! Other clan members that were keeping watch over the refuge cave system alerted the whole Clan spread throughout the extended caves and crevices that she had returned after several weeks! And, most importantly, Beeshmah had succeeded in getting *all* the synthetic humanoids (except for Majoreen, whom was on an extended mission) to join the coalition!

This was confirmed by Dominionists Clan Chief Rhett—for *his* own two specialists, Maajida an Preun and Laray Salomenes, who had accompanied Beeshmah on the mission, had reported to the chief the success of their task. Rhett simply sent one of his clanfolk over to the Vestigians' caves to tell Councilor Thuall in person… This, of course, was all necessary so that the humans would not use their frequency communiques and be detected by the aliens.

Besides the verification sent by Chief Rhett, Beeshmah was able to show vid recordings of parts of their endeavor to the Councilor and the rest of the Clan.

JOSETH MOORE

The Clan was able to share Beeshmah's vid recordings in an intra-comm system—very similar the way the synthetic humanoids were able to communicate with each other when they were a few feet from one another. However, Miriana insisted that they gathered around each other while different clan members passed Beeshmah's device around so everyone else could watch portions of the mission themselves...Miriana simply did not want to take any chances of being detected by the crawlers!

The verifications were needed since Number 4 was *not* there with her! Beeshmah informed the large gathering of the Vestige Clan what Number 4's new plan was, at the suggestion of the humans. That is, following the quadrawalkers to see where the aliens' base or mothership was located on cMaj!

Also, since Number 4's team felt it would have been too much of an emotional shock to *all* the clandoms to have the two synthetics show up *within* their caves during such a trying time of hiding from the aliens, they all thought it was a good idea for Forward On and Ascent to *remain* in their own caves for the time being. But later, Miriana, again, insisted that she wanted *her* entire Clan to *meet* them—psychological discomfort or not! For the alliance was formed for an existential reason, *not* as a club, she would tell the Vestigians a few times!

On the Dominionists' side of things, Maajida and Laray debriefed their Clan leader. Rhett's style of governing was far different from Miriana's. After the two young specialists returned to *their* refuge cave system, Chief Rhett clandestinely routed them to a private section of *their* cave system that most of the Dominionists members knew nothing about! It was there that the two specialists informed and showed their own recordings from the mission to Rhett and what their plans, with Number 4, were in dealing with the aliens…

The Maji were also informed about the plans from, both, Number 4's team and Councilor Thuall's strategy that she and her small circle of advisors came up with in utilizing the starship's crash site! Even though the cMaji tiny clandom did not possess any type of enforcement organization in their Settlement, they were still part of the coalition of humans and synthetics. So, they had to be informed of the plans. Miriana and Rhett, both, sent their own messengers to the Maji leader and close cousin to Miriana, Caradoc Sohill.

Finally, it was the first time that humans felt some kind of security since the arrival of the aliens, now that the alliance's plans and members had *all* consolidated into the *same* region of the cave systems and bluffs of the humans' refuge zone!

With the exception of the Maji, all the humans had hastened the cobbling of new weapons they could scrounge up from the stone all around them within the cave and bluff systems!

The human population on cMaj actually had history books, thanks to Miriana's mother's foresight from decades ago! The Vestigians and Dominionists referred to some of the captured historical events on war—for, Miriana's generation was a population not familiar with proper war. They were used to *skirmishes* between humans and the rogue synths, and even between the different Clans! But, as one of the sections in one of the history books made reference to in the religious portion: It was a David and Goliath prospect...

No one knew, exactly, what that meant—not even the synthetic humanoids with their extensive actuary intelligence! For their initial programming was only as good as the information that was feed *to* them. And the deepest of human history was lost not only due to the destruction of the generational starship, Vestige, but also due to the simple entropy of Time itself!

CHAPTER FORTY-THREE

A few days passed by since Beeshmah, Maajida, and Laray had returned to the refuge zone with Ascent and Forward On. The two human-like mechanicals' reception from all three Clans was considerably cool. It was to be expected. For, aside from human emotions about the history of the events of the Rebellion of the synthetics, there was the real and present situation of being prepared for the possibility of war with the aliens.

Councilor Housenn Thuall didn't expect a welcoming disposition from the Clans. Even the cMaji kept a bit of distance from Forward On and Ascent! Indeed, it was telling just how deep the collective and historical memory was of the Rebellion.

Again, everything that all the humans, and even the synthetics, were going through was because of that fateful day of Singularity when *some* of the synthetics on starship Vestige *and* on the planet of cMaj and its three moons, had decided to *forcibly* tip the societal balance to *their* favor... or die in trying to do so.

Deep within one of the cave system's largest pocket of space, during the most recent of an all–clandom gatherings, Councilor Housenn Thuall stated that it was *another* point of Singularity! But that time, it was with the convergence of the human and synthetic coalition against that of the aliens! In her speech to, literally, every human being that was left on cMaj, she told them that they should learn from the oral *and* written history about not only the Synthetics' Rebellion, but of the history of many other swings of balance throughout humanity.

After she gave her speech, the Councilor gave way from the roughly-hewn lectern so that Lanay Thuall— that surviving pilot, and *last* survivor, that had landed the ship that would eventually lead to Mirana's generation, could address the entire human species.

The all-clan gathering was meant to be a call to arms. The humans weren't sure when the aliens would reach them. But given the proximity of their eerily crawling probes, they were not far behind!

Lanay, assisted by an adolescent Maji, leaned against the outcrop-turned-into-lectern. She started her speech before the 250 or so humans, packed into the large cave that was lit by energized solar voltaic lamps, when a low, long rumbling started...

Panic began to ensue! All three Clans recognized the tremor: it was from the aliens' great spaceship that had passed by each of their caves at one point or another!

And, so the battle begins, Miriana thought to herself as she looked upon the screaming and sobbing humans before her! She directed a couple of young members of her own extended family to help take Lanay to safety and then she ran over to Ascent and Forward On! Filleppe, Fillamon, and most of Miriana's own family converged around the Councilor as she met the two synthetics!

"Looks like we can't wait for Number 4 to get back from his task," Councilor Thuall shouted to the mechanicals over the sea of voices! "Now's the time to utilize your skills that you used during the Rebellion, my friends!"

Ascent and Forward On nodded at her in unison, and actually said to her for the first time, "Yes, Councilor!"

As Councilor Thuall, Chief Rhett, and Leader Caradoc, all, positioned themselves around the lectern and bellowed at the clandoms to calm down and take up their arms, the two *allied* synths ignited their rockets and lifted themselves above the crowd of humans! Both held up their hands in a calming gesture to the roiling humans!

"Colonists," Forward On spoke, "now is the time to gather your thoughts, your weapons, and to implement the plans you've talked about for several weeks, now..."

The rumbling stopped!

Despite what Forward On said, *and* despite *all* the planning and gathering of weapons, and everything else; in the end, most of the humans were simply too scared to do much against any oncoming foe at that point!

But there was a small number of brave ones among the humans—from *all* Clans, even a few from the cMaj! They had their sharpened stone spears and daggers, their taut projectile-shooters, and even simple loose stone on hand to throw at the aliens!

Then a series of lights flashed from outside the large cave's mouth and into the dim cavern. It shone against the humans, causing a gradual calm among them! There was something very familiar about it. Indeed, reassuring.

The lights flashed: *We come in peace...*

Just then, Councilor Housenn Thuall noticed that the two allied synthetics flinched and looked at each other! Within the, now, quieted cave, Miriana ran over to Forward On and Ascent!

"What is it," she asked with a countenance of confusion!

Both synthetics' rocket jets, audibly, slowed in intensity as the mechanicals lowered themselves to the cave's floor. The two synthetic beings looked at each other in wonderment.

"Stars, would someone please tell me what's going on," Councilor Thuall finally shouted anyone who would provide an answer!

"Miri!"

The deep, scratchy mechanical voice that echoed was that of Number 4! Every human in the chamberesque cave turned their heads to him, as he stood at the opening; one of his hands held out in a beckoning gesture to her, specifically.

"My child...you must come now, and bring everyone with you..."

The Councilor looked wild-eyed at her husband and their adult children, and their children! A confused murmuring was slowly rising among the humans in the expansive cave.

"Councilor," Ascent said to her softly, a hand placed gently on one of her shoulders, "it's going to be alright now...come on! All of you...single-file, please!"

"And you won't need your weapons," Number 4 threw out over the rising voices in the cave. "It's time for you to go home!"

"—what?"

"—did, did he just say what I think he said?"

"—maybe it's a trap!"

"—I'm scared!"

Despite themselves, the homo sapiens followed the Councilor, her family, and Number 4 as they all filed out of the cave. Ascent and Forward On stood at either side of the cave's mouth, directing the long stream of humans out of the cave...

To their absolute amazement, the giant ship that had been such consternation to them for long weeks was, now, silently hovering above the flatten land directly outside the large cave system! It was, indeed, long and cylindrical and had a series of smaller ships descending from its ventral section...

Councilor Thuall and Filleppe had to be pulled along by their grandchildren, as they both gawked at the 600-or so foot spaceship! Her generation, with the exception of Lanay Thuall, had *never* seen anything of technology so big in their lives before—with the exception of historic vids that Number 4 had shown them with his projections! Behind Miriana's immediate family, all the other humans were finally making their way out of the cave and many having the very same reaction as the Housenn Thualls!

Finally, the Councilor's eyes looked below the behemoth and saw scores of quadrawalkers! But they were, as it were, standing at attention, as if they were soldiers making way for their leader.

And, indeed, there was a young woman in uniform, quickly walking with a large entourage—a young, *human* woman, with an entourage of *other humans*...

While she was walking toward the Councilor, not too far from the small ship the young woman and her team had debarked, the cobbled airship of the once-rogue synths had landed. It was synthetic laborer Number 2—otherwise known as Majoreen! Also present were all the ships from the three clandoms. They were parked, their pilots standing next to them and in conversation with the other humans! The exception being Number 4's ship, as he was ushering the long line of humans from the cave.

The young woman with the entourage finally made it up to where Councilor Thuall and her family were. In the midst of the cacophony surrounding Miriana, the young woman unexpectedly stopped—as did the other humans surrounding her, in matching uniforms! She snapped up her right hand—palm flat and fingers together and pointed upward, in front and next to her right shoulder!

"Commander Svana Quispe of the search and rescue team, from the starship Vasculum Fugae! Several years ago, our ship had detected an explosion above the atmosphere of this planet and was able to trace the trajectory to that of our mothership. I am informed that you are one of the authorities on the planet of cMaj, and I hereby offer my assistance for the rescue of the citizens, or offspring of the citizens, of starship Vestige…"

Fin

Printed in the United States
by Baker & Taylor Publisher Services